# 50 SHADES OF
# SCOTLAND

# MICHAEL KELLY

# 50 SHADES OF SCOTLAND

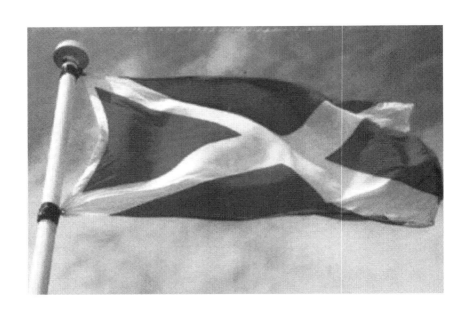

# MICHAEL KELLY

PUBLISHED BY BIG IDEAS PUBLICATIONS

2.GREENSIDE LESLIE. FIFE.SCOTLAND

Other Novels by Michael Kelly available on your Amazon Kindle.

# 50 SHADES OF SCOTLAND

## HOLLYWOOD..LOS ANGELES...U.S.A.. FEBUARY 2018..

## CHAPTER 1

## FUCK ME.

*"Fuck me"* !! Madonna screamed in that annoying American accent everybody's trying to imitate these days..... *"Fuck me"* !!!

*"Who are you wanting to fuck you now.. You old Hoor"* .?? Rita Ora asked in her fake American accent.... Copying Madonna..

*"That Dude there"* Madge pointed... *"Look"*..

Rita put down the Grass joint she was building and has a wee squint over so as she could get a better look at the screen of Madge's tablet.. Her jaw nearly hit the floor '' *Oh.. My Gawd''*.. She gasped .. She speaks in that annoying fake accent most of the way through the story...Except when her and Madonna are practicing there Skattish accents that is.. But you'll hear all about that in just a wee while. .For now though. .It's that fake Yankee.. Doodle Dandy accent she's speaking in... *"Oh .My .Gawd" Sh*e gasped and licked her lips. ..... *" I'd get my gums around his plums alright.... Who is it"?*

*"He lives in Leslie"* Was Madonna's answer..

Before I tell you what was causing all the stooshie. .I'll tell you the story about how the two pals reached this point.. Imagine if you can, the pair of them sitting in Madonna's flat and Madge asking Rita if she would ride that Hunk whose near naked. Kilted torso was smiling out at them from the screen of her tablet
They weren't looking at the Porn websites again. .I can tell you that much..

## CHAPTER 2

## THE STORY

Here's how the story goes... Things were looking rosy for the two Gals at long last you see..... .Oh yeah. .Rosy indeed... And not before time either.. Because things hadn't been so good since'' *Kettyfill''*  The local paper mill, had closed down .

They'd both worked in the Bag Factory department of the paper mill since leaving school......

Madge had worked there for 15 years.. While Rita had gave them 9 years service.... . Then one morning. .Nearly 4 years ago.. The Managers had walked in and told them all the Mill was shutting down. .And that was it...They were landed *''On The Dole''* for the first time in their lives...The redundancy money never lasted long either. .Not long at all.. Most of that had went up in smoke.. Literally.. Up in smoke...Because with having all that spare money to throw about... They could afford to buy even more weed every single week. .And fair enough. .The Dole had tried to get them to take other jobs...But stacking shelves at their local branch of Lidl or Aldi or working in McDonalds wasn't for these Gals...No Siree... Some of the jobs were away in another part of California altogether. One such job was working in an Amazon fulfilment centre...  Nearly 30 miles away from Hollywood. .Amazon seemingly laid on a bus for their workers   But even that would mean more than an hour's travelling each morning ….Then work a 12 hour shift… Then spend another hour getting home in the evening..??.     .A 14 hour day ?  Every single day of the week.. For what?. .The pay was only minimum wage… Volunteering in charity shops wouldn't exactly full-fill the Gals potential either…Na. .Na. .

They weren't scared of work…But for the moment.. They were better off on the Dole… Getting up to a wee scam or two…Or they could always get a wee turn at one of the lap dancing clubs away down in Florida Keys again…. You had to watch yourself at that though. .Because.. There was always somebody in Hollywood ready to grass you to the D.S.S .. *(Department Of Social Security..)*  The Dole. .Aye ..There was always somebody. .Jealous because they think you're getting something they're not..

There was one funny incident. .Just the other month. .When Rita had been grassed …And hauled into the D.S.S offices.. They thought they had caught her at the Lap dancing.  Aye. .They thought they had her well and truly nabbed….But she'd got away with it.. Oh yeah.. .It was a scream…A scream indeed. .And maybe I'll tell you all about it later on?. .It all depends..

Before things had turned so Rosy.. They had seriously thought about getting back into the scamming …. Catalogue's mostly. .Because just before Rita had moved across the landing from Madge. .They'd been onto a good thing with the Catalogues.... .And I'll tell you a wee bit about how that and a few other scams all came to be...And it'll give you a wee bit of insight about how Barry Bang Bang came to find out about the size of the attic in the house she was in now... You've not heard anything about Barry Bang Bang. .But you'll hear more about him and his crazy gang of sisters shortly.....

But…. Anyway……Rita had met this Dude on the Plenty Of Fish website…        His name was Justin… .Justin Timberlake. .His P.O.F. profile said he was a musician.....Only 3 weeks into the romance, she'd jacked in the flat she had and moved in with Justin.. But it turned out he was a pervert...Then after only 4 months, Justin had suddenly announced that he was chucking her….

He said he needed some space...Some space to full-fill his creative potential.....Write and record his own songs he'd told her...  A lot of shite…

Rita knew fine well he was lying and the real reason he was chucking her was…. Rita wouldn't smear her fanny with peanut butter and let him video ''*Sabre*'' his pit bull terrier licking the peanut butter off.. He'd promised her the video would be private and he wouldn't put in on the W.W.W for all to see..

She told him she would do anything for love...But she won't do that.. No way... It was a different story altogether when Rita had suggested that Justin should try it first....He should smear the peanut butter all over his cock and balls. .And let *"Sabre"* lick it off. .Aye.. That was a different story,, He wouldn't do it.. Naw..Would he hell. .And Rita knew the reason for that as well... Sabre had teeth like a fuckin; shark and Justin was scared.. Scared in case Sabre took a bite instead of a lick.. He was scared of getting a vasectomy in one foul bite.... Scared...And no matter how much Justin pleaded.. She wasn't covering her fanny in peanut butter and letting his dog lick it off...

.That was one reason he'd chucked her and fine she knew it....

The other reason was she wouldn't shave her fanny for him again...

She'd done it for him once. .But never again.....Fair enough.. She had made a great big.. Big mistake, whilst doing this the first time.  But it didn't matter. ..She wasn't doing it again... Justin had been on and on and on and on at her you see...Begging her to shave her fanny for him.. Then he told her that if she really truly loved him?. .She would do it.. She'd never done this for any man before. Ever... .But after weeks and weeks of him harping on,. She'd gave in and agreed.... She'd nipped through to Justin's lavvie and had got to work with the Gillette...She

11

didn't have much of a clue at all, but eventually.. She finished. Everything was braw and smooth, if you know what I mean ?   But the great big.. Big mistake she made was... She'd splashed a big handful of Justin's after shave on her bare Toosh....She'd never even took a thought...But you talk about scream?  ...You'd have thought somebody was trying to Murder her.. And you talk about hot ??  ?..You'd have thought somebody was at her fanny with blowtorch...... I'm sure you can just picture her ..Screaming like a stuck pig. .Dancing jumping and hopping about Justin's lavvie like she was in''*Riverdance*'' and walking like Frankenstein over to Justin's sink.. .It didn't matter how much cold water she'd splashed between her legs though. Her Muff had been roasting hot....She'd been walking like John Wayne for days....And if that wasn't bad and bad enough.. She couldn't get riding for a good wee while after the experience with the after shave... .Justin hadn't been happy about that either...

Then of course.. She had nearly clawed the fanny off herself altogether when her pubic hair had started growing back in again..

.Perhaps if you're a woman reading this and you've ever got to work with the Gillette.? Then you'll know exactly how Rita felt with the scratch.. Scratch. Scratching..........

But he'd chucked her...Rita had even suggested that she could maybe be a backing singer if Justin managed to record anything?.. He wasn't up for this at all..

Then she said they could both write songs together .?..He didn't fancy that idea either..

Aye...Justin had chucked her.....And the sonofabitch had chucked her out his pad as well...So Rita managed to find a private let...It was a poky wee damp, one bedroom flat.. In another part of town altogether...Over on West 34.. . The old lady who lived there before Rita got the flat. .A Mrs Angela Black.. Had stayed there for 40 odd years...Until her family put her in an old folk's home... This lady had been one of the old school. .Honest as the day was long...And as the letters from the Gas Board. The Electricity board ..Banks Etc  Etc proved.. This elderly lady had everything paid up front...Never any debt.. Which meant the house wasn't blacklisted ...

And that was very handy  ..Because with Madge being a material girl and also that bit older and therefor more wordily wise than Rita...She'd told Rita it was Justin's loss....She had also put Rita on to a scam.....And that scam was...

As long as your address wasn't blacklisted...You could phone up the Next catalogue....And they would deliver $4oo worth of anything you fancied out the catalogue,

13

straight to your front door the following day...They would... .And it maybe sounds terrible...But that's just exactly what they had done....Next would send even more goodies if you made a payment or two. .But these Gals had no intention of paying anything...Not a bolt. .

There was always plenty more catalogues.. Plenty more.. They had both been swanning about town dressed up in the best of gear... .Looking just like the models from these catalogues... They had indeed. .Ray Ban sunglasses ..Le Coq Sportiff trainers...A brand new watch each... Braw new denim mini-skirts.. Three or four pairs of shag me High Heels each.. They had ordered braw boots for the winter and a couple of braw new warm winter coats each as well......

.Everything the catalogues would be kind enough to send them.. Rita had only been in that flat for 8 months before she got word of a council house....Right across the landing from Madonna...Madge was more excited than Rita when she'd heard the good news...Because Madge would be able to keep an eye on Rita.  Keep her out of trouble.. Keep her on the right path so to speak.. Be a mother figure to the girl ??  ....  Although with Rita moving from the private let.. That meant an end to the scamming with the catalogues. .And the name Angela Black left behind... But with Madge keeping Rita on the right path...She'd managed to convince her there was one more scam they could pull before she moved home... Bright-House !!!!

Madge had managed to convince Rita this was a magic idea..

All that brand new gear for my brand new home Rita had asked when coming round to the idea?....But this wasn't Madge's plan. .Oh no, Christ no... Madge had a plan to get some ready cash...Cash on the nose.. A magic idea... And at the local branch of Bright house... Angela Black had got the latest 60 inch smart television.. The latest all singing. .All dancing washing machine...A beautiful dishwasher... Rita...Or Angela didn't like to go over the score in Bright-House.. Didn't want to knock the arse right out of things. .If you know what I mean ?. So she got a 3 piece suite into the bargain. .And that was to be it .But Madge had convinced her to get a Dyson Hoover as well. .And a cracking Hi-Fi..

Thousands upon thousands of Dollars worth of the latest gear...All on easy weekly payment terms. .Aye right..??..Bright-house weren't getting paid a bolt either. No way ...Not a bolt....And two days later... When the delivery drivers had been carrying the brand new stuff from Bright-House through Rita's. .Or Angela Blacks front door.. The delivery drivers didn't know, There was another two delivery drivers. .Just waiting to take most of the gear straight out the back door. . Straight out the back door and into George Naylor's white transit van.. When I say most of the gear.. That's not strictly true.. Because….With Madge being a material girl.. She had convinced Rita just to gift the Dyson Hoover to her…After all.. Rita wouldn't have all that lovely cash from George if Madge hadn't thought of the scam in the first place…The least Rita could do was gift her bestest pal the Dyson.. .Surely. ..Madge promised Rita that she could have a wee shot of the Dyson any time she wanted. Anytime.. .That's what bestest pals were for, wasn't it.? . Sharing is caring as Madge had put it….Apart from the Dyson.. Madge would also be entitled to claim half the money Rita had got from George for all the goodies from Bright-House . Surely ??… .He'd paid half price for everything…….It was Madge who had set it all up with George   Wasn't it ? The very least Rita could do was share the cash with her very bestest pal. .Wasn't it ??     Sharing is caring Madge had repeated..

One of the pair of delivery drivers helping George collect the goodies from Brighthouse had been his part time girlfriend.. Barry Bang  Bangs older sister…. Moira…Who of course was curious as to where Rita was flitting to..??..Rita had told her innocently she had got a flat in the same block as Madge…In fact…It was straight across the landing from Madge.. Moira had asked if it was a top floor flat. ??   It was indeed  ….Even though the flats were only two stories high.. It was a top floor flat………

*"Interesting"* was all Moira had said.. *"Very interesting indeed"*.. Moira had even volunteered to help George with the removals when the time came for Rita to move to her new home... .And she done just that..

The first thing she had done after she'd carried a table lamp up the stairs to Rita's new house was to tell Rita that she wanted a look at her attic. .When she found out the size of it.. She had told Madge she wanted a look up into her attic as well. *"Very handy indeed"* she'd said. .''Very handy indeed"......

From hearing the above stories about the scamming Etc....You might have run away with the idea that Rita was being led astray by Madonna.. Taken by the hand and manipulated into doing whatever Madge wanted her to. .Although this was partly true.. And Rita would be the first to admit this.. But then again. On the other hand....The way Rita looked at things   It was an Education....Madge was just learning her. .Learning her just how fly folk could be.. Because with Rita having a rather sheltered childhood... Being brought up on a smallholding on the outskirts of Hollywood, she was a country Gal really, and wasn't up to all these tricks. .Wasn't all that streetwise would be a better way of putting it. ..She was fairly getting her eyes open though.. Oh yeah. .And if Mommy and Pappy were ever hearing about the scams with Brighthouse or even worse, what they were getting up to for Barry Bang.. Bang. .Gee !!  They would disown her altogether.. It was bad enough when the minister's wife had caught Rita riding the minister of their church... ..Mom And Pops had been so embarrassed by that particular affair. They had stopped going to church for more than a year.....

Behind her parents backs.. The locals in her Hamlet had named that incident. .The case of *"The Vicar In The Vestry"*..

The Gals had seriously planned to send away for a provisional driving licence with the money they'd got from George...Then they had planned to take an intensive driving course...Get through their driving tests double quick...Then they'd both get a wee second hand car each....A shaggin' wagon each...Fuckin' braw......And It's not as if the girls couldn't be bothered doing all this... .... But  Well...By the time they'd treated themselves to an ounce of weed each. They figured it might be better just to make the very best of the ready cash they had and wait until another time to take the intensive driving course so as they could get through their driving tests ....So they had just bought another ounce of weed and imagined what kind of shaggin' wagon they were going to buy....

Some of their other friends had told them about another scam.. A scam to get even more money from the dole for doing fuck all.....

It was a thing called D..L. A. ( *Disability Living allowance* ) But some of things you had to do and say   Just to scam your way onto this particular benefit. ?  .Well.?  They were just ridiculous..... .Scandalous and absolutely shameless..

One of their pals called Brittany Spears had told the D.S.S. she was unfit to work because she pished and shat the bed every single night.... She'd even done the old trick with the miniature bottle filled with water at the interview????

Another friend...Lady Ga Ga ..Well..?   She'd went Ga..Ga Altogether   In the Dole office.. She'd grabbed one of the interviewees by the throat ..She'd called the woman Poker Face as she pulled her across the desk and told her she couldn't work because of the violent fantasies she was experiencing..  Liable tae dae some Hoor in she'd said. .Lady Ga  Ga also told the woman that if she stopped her money?. .Then Lady Ga Ga would stop her breath... They'd phoned the police for Lady Ga Ga again that time.. She'd got on the D.L A though..

Another friend they knew...Shakira..... .She got herself an invisible dog ...She did ..Honestly....It was a black and white collie...It's mum and dad were both sheepdogs she told folk.. And she had named the Collie'' *Patch"*. She told Patch to sit when she was going into the shops and everything...She even went around her neighbours

19

apologising for Patch barking through the night...But as you already know.. .Shakira was just letting on that she was round the twist. Away with the Fairies......Just to scam her way onto the old D.L.A.... And some of the things other pals had told the D.S.S ?..They were even a match. .For Patch...

The girls wouldn't even be considering any of these ideas...No siree... Especially since things had turned out so rosy for the pair of them..

Before the paper mill had closed down and the two Gals had took up the scamming.. Them and some other friends had often been on drunken nights in some the many Karaoke bars that were in Hollywood at one time. .Some of these friends had said the pair was no' bad chanters on the old Karaoke.....     A few of these friends had suggested they should maybe try for the X factor or maybe even America's got talent..?    And of course the girls had seriously thought about this idea many times.. Oh yeah. They both had fantasies about being famous pop stars.. Or glamour Models...Oh they had often Imagined themselves on the Telly...Like most Gals I suppose??... None of the pair of them had taken this thought any further though.  .But it was still an option...

They had to put scamming the catalogues behind them after Rita moved house And although that was a big set back.....Things had still turned rosy for the pair of them...Rosy indeed...They were loaded and would be even more loaded next week... .Because ..Just yesterday..., Madge had won a whack of money on a lucky number 7 scratch-card.... Almost 3 thousand Dollars she'd won..... The money would be in her bank account later on today or tomorrow.....

Rita. Meanwhile. .She'd got 3 and a half thousand Dollars back from a miss-sold P.P. I. claim.. That meant they had nearly $6.500 between them at the minute......Things were looking rosy indeed for the two Gals.. And like I told you just a wee while ago... Things would be looking even rosier next week.... They'd have even more cash next week.. Another 6.500 Dollars each next week...That meant they would have 19 and a half thousand Dollars between them...Aye..19 and a half thousand.... And the reason they'd have all this lovely cash is. .....They had both rented there attics out to one of Hollywood's craziest men... Barry Bang Bang.. Barry wasn't living in the attic though. .Oh no. .No. .No. Christ no.. When George Naylor's part time girlfriend and delivery driver... .Barry's sister.. Moira... Had told Barry about Rita moving across the landing from Madge. .And all about the size of their attics ...Barry also found this information to be '' *Very Interesting* ''.

 Rita had only been in her new flat for 3 nights when Barry and a younger crazy sister.. Mary, had paid a visit while

Rita and Madge had both been watching Coronation Street ..After checking out the attics for himself... .He'd made them both an offer they couldn't refuse. ....

*"Get the attics Filt "* had been his offer..*"Stappitt Foo"*... It was an offer they had thought they had better not refuse.. Cause Barry's four sisters were every bit as crazy as Barry. .Every bit...

Barry had easily convinced  them they were onto a sure fire winner. All that lovely cash  Right on the nose.. Every three months..Lovely..Jubbley...  He had asked his sister Mary, to back him up.. And you know what she said.. Don't you ? .

Remember.. Barry's sisters were every bit as crazy as him..

In fact. The second oldest of the Bang Bang sisters ...Jean.. Was in the penitentiary at the minute,,.. A  7 years sentence for attempted murder. .She'd tried to do somebody in. .Somebody who thought they would be smart and try to rip Barry off for some of his crop. ..But the other 3 sisters were still going about...

 Everything had been organised with the tanks. .Lights Etc for the following evening... And before they knew what was really happening...  .Both Madge and Rita were growing 26 grass plants in their attics for Barry Bang Bang and his band of crazy sisters. .Barry had even been kind enough to rig both their Electricity meters for them.

."*Watch this*" He'd told them. .And as if by magic.. The wheel on their Electric meter had stopped turning round altogether...Magical indeed....

.He'd also showed them what to do when the Electric man was due to come round and read their meters... That had been just over 3 months ago... ...The crop was ready.. Cut down and next week.. When it was completely dried out altogether......One of Barry's crazy sisters would be round to collect the lot and hopefully...Hopefully...Drop off the spondoolies... .6.500 Dollars each. .In cash.... .6.500 Dollars guaranteed every three months Barry had promised them...But if the sister decided not to pay ?..Then well..???..They'd cross that bridge if it came to it. .But attempting to kick fuck out that sister would not be a wise option.. This is one of the reasons why they would each be keeping a wee bit of the crop to themselves.. Not a lot.. Well .Not an awful lot. ..About a Quarter of an ounce each up until now.....Barry would never miss that off all these plants.. Would he ?..

Would he ???

 Even though what they were smoking off his crop at the minute had been dried in Madge's Microwave earlier on that day... .It wasn't a bad smoke at all...Not bad for first timers...Anyway.. They'd have to explain to Barry's sister.... Or rather ..They would have to ask Barry's sisters permission.      They'd ask If it was O.K to cancel the start of the next crop for three weeks or so ? .....Barry would understand. ?

Surely...?

Hopefully. ?   .

He'd understand that with the girls never having so much ready cash to spend since they'd got their redundancy money from the paper mill.... They were desperate to get away somewhere exotic... .A wee vacation... Away from the Rat Race. ...As they would explain...Looking after 26 grass plants in the attic for 3 months is hard. .Time consuming work indeed...It's a full time job. .

And if you have ever been into that game, then you'll know how time consuming it can be...

Up and down the ladders to the attic.. Every single night to check the P.H levels...

You'll know all about the water having to be changed every so often.

You'll know all about the hose leading down from the attic into the bucket ?

Remember. .The Gals had 26 plants growing in their each individual attics...26 plants..5 six foot tanks. That's an awful lot of water to get up and down your attic.. And then you've to get the old water back down.....

You'll know all about having to cut the shaders off the plants.. Then of course. You have to look out for the dreaded spider mite..

And of course...With the Gals being new to the game... Pure amateurs.... That made things all the more difficult..

Time consuming work indeed..

Then you have all the worry about whether the neighbours or the postman can smell the weed..?  .

 If you have ever been into this game yourself?   Then you'll know fine about the fear of the police finding out all about your plantation...And taking all your lovely wee Babies away eh ?..Sha Hoor Sir.. Nobodies wantin' that ..Eh no ?

Both girls found the old paranoia was also very stress-full.. They were both totally shitting themselves every time they heard a car drawing up outside or there was a knock at the door .Thinking.... This is it.. Bust.. .But the end result would be well worth it......Wouldn't it ? ...  An extra 6.500 Dollars each for them to spend ?  Every 3 months.....They deserved a break didn't they ??    .. And they were planning the vacation of a lifetime.. Of a fuckin' lifetime.. And at this very moment that's just exactly what they were doing.... Sitting in Madge's flat again... Getting stoned on Barry Bang Bangs weed and searching through the Internet pages. .Finding out all they could about the place they had decided to go on vacation for a few weeks...Somewhere they could blaw every single Cent of their hard earned cash...Somewhere they could both get the Arse rodgered right aff themselves.. It was a shag fest they were going on.. A fuckin' well shag Fest...

They'd have plenty more cash the next time they grew another crop for Barry Bang.Bang  anyway..6.500 Dollars each...Wouldn't they??.

.Christ.. They could be away a vacation every other 3 months..If Barry Bang  Bang would be so understanding..??  If he would be kind enough to give them the time off so to speak ??              But remember ..It's one of Hollywood's craziest men we're talking about here..

The Gals had discussed the idea of them both going to Ibiza?.. But they wanted to go somewhere nobody else in this one horse town they call Hollywood had ever been......And that's what this town was turning into. .A one horse town...Where the horse has already left.. Everything shutting down. .Most of the pubs.. Most of the clubs. .It was all Kebab shops  Charity shops.. Chinese carry out shops. .Hairdressers and beauty salons in Hollywood High Street nowadays...Oh yeah...And two Tattooists as well... And an Undertakers as into the bargain. .All that was missing was the tumbleweed blowing about the street...It was a boring place to live now.. A ghost town... Even the local town hall had shut down. .Not like in Hollywood's Hey-Day. .When great Rock and Roll bands such as *"The Skids"* had played there..

The girls had toyed with the plan of going to Shagaluff ? ...But they wanted to go somewhere truly special..

They had thought about heading to Goa?  But Goa didn't sound exotic enough..

They had fantasies about the two of them taking off on a round the world cruise..

And these places and plans were all good and well.. They'd find plenty Cock in all these places. .Oh yeah

Rita had suggested Ireland. ..We can do Saint Patricks day in Buncrana she'd said.......Have a competition to see who can get shagged the most...??.

Because these Gals experience with Irishmen had taught them that. .Although they are amongst the proudest hard working men they've ever met.... After their working day is over. .All these Irishmen really cared about was. .A Right Good Feed. .A Right Good Drink and a Right Good Royde. .Not always necessarily in that order.

But ...  When they stumbled across the City Of Leslie website. .All these other plans had swiftly went right oot the windae..

Leslie it was for these pair.. Leslie  Skatland as Madge had said in her American accent. ...Situated just below the Lomond hills...The twin peaks of The Kingdom Of Fife... She'd said this in an American accent as well.... It was on the East Lomond Hill where the legendry 20 foot high letters stood... ..The 20 foot high letters you often saw at the start of many famous Movies...The 20 foot high letters proclaiming..

### 'LESLIE'

They could also do Saint Patricks day in Skatland.   Marry the two ideas into one...Because Leslie also held the biggest Saint Patricks day parade outside the Island of Ireland....

They had read on the city of Leslie website that the Leslie City council turned the three rivers that flow through the city...Green....The River Leven. .The River Lothrie and the Cammy Burn    All turned Green.. Just to celebrate the glorious occasion...And apart from the flute bands and the pipe bands that swarmed to Leslie from as far away as North Africa. .Canada    Nova Scotia. Jamaica. And Switzerland...They also expected an influx of over a Million visitors to the City for the week long celebration of Irelands legendary Saint....

They had watched the video of last year's march on You Tube .It had boasted that if you stood at the one spot.

.The parade would take six hours to pass you.. .And right enough.. The Rivers had all been turned Green....They'd watched as The City Mayor... Ryan Boyle, had proudly lead the parade, which started at the Prinlaws quarter of the City. .On to Leslie Boulevard itself....It had snaked through the University and the Harbour areas before finally ending up at the Greenside quarter...And there was a lot of folk right enough..

Ryan Boyle was to lead the parade again this year...Despite last year's unsuccessful attempt on his life .. The would be assassin was never caught.. Rumours had been rife at the time that one of the many Leslie crime cartels had hired the world famous Hit-Man.  Known only as ''*Grey-Cloud* to shoot The City Mayor.

Some say it was some certain Leslie children themselves who had saved up all their dinner money and hired the Gunman?..

The rumour had been the children were totally fed up with Ryan shouting at them for drawing houses with all different colours of chalk on the pavements of the street he lived. .An area of Leslie known as The Bowery Quarter.. ...

This was after Ryan had made sure every single member of his government were trained how to react if there was a nuclear war. .A major plane crash or a Tsunami in Leslie.

.Yep.. A Tsunami..( *Even though Leslie was 9 miles away from the sea* )....But if there is ever a nuclear war.. A Tsunami.. Or a major plane crash in the area ? Then the good citizens of Leslie were simply to go and knock Ryan's door.. He'll gladly advise you on how to react....

Ryan had been going absolutely crazy at the children on that first evening, when he'd caught them drawing houses with all different colours of chalk.. Mad he'd been going.. Around the twist altogether..

*''Help ma Boab !!''* He'd shouted. .*''Help ma Boab !!!!'*

Even Ryan's trusty body guard....His black Labrador *''Cindy''* had barked twice, not only with shock and horror. .But keeping in mind, that if she kept on Daddy's good side. Then he might treat her to some strawberry flavoured Yoghurt when they got home..?

You might not believe this. .But it's true... Some of these children who were chalking on the pavement were even as old as 7 years old. ..

And Ryan had used his fingers to count of all the different colours of chalk to the children..

*''Blue chalk''* !!!..Ryan had pointed with his walking stick at the blue house...This particular house had pink smoke coming from the chimney. .And a big smiling yellow sun chalked in the sky above it..

*''White chalk !!!* He'd screamed and pointed at the white house with the tree drawn in front of it...In brown chalk...

*''Pink chalk'' !!!* He'd roared and pointed his walking stick at the pink house with the green two wheeled car drawn in front of it.

*"Orange chalk''!!!..* He'd pointed his walking stick at the orange house with all the windows in place. .A door. .But without a roof on it.. But with three or four different colours of matchstick men and woman standing on a path outside ..The path was drawn in purple..

*"Brown chalk'' !!!*

*"Green chalk'' !!*

*"Purple chalk ''!!* He'd been blue in the face and foaming at the mouth by the time he'd counted off all the different colours of chalk....

And as for *''Cindy''*??..Well. *.''Cindy'..'* Had barked another six or seven times in agreement...She was still thinking about the treat Daddy might give her when they got home. .The strawberry flavoured Yoghurt.

Ryan asked the children to imagine what would happen if there was a Tsunami?. .A major plane crash?. Or a Nuclear war in the area?..

''You''ll all be dead.. That's what would happen'' He screamed at these children..'' Dead !!  .. Fried to death or drowned''...

''And all you've got to do is draw houses on pavements'' He'd screamed..   ''With all those different colours of chalk.. Every colour of chalk under the sun'' ???

 A lot of these children had just stood open mouthed in disbelief. .Some of them were even crying.. Not even a word of apology though.. Not a word.. ? Ha..

So in reply to these children's insubordination...Ryan had been shouting and screaming at them it was 20 lashes of the Birch they were needing...

He'd screamed at the children they were out of parental control.. Rebels.. And if they didn't break this cycle of Anti- Social behaviour?.. Then they'd all grow up to be Rapists and Murderers and Drug Addicts...

He also told them Santa Clause wasn't real..

.Oh aye. .It was Ryan Boyle they were dealing with here boy...

He'd told them it was their mums and dads. .Not Santa Clause at all....

Even though these children had all been crying their wee hearts out by this time... ...Ryan couldn't show weakness...That wasn't Ryan's way..

Do you think he had been voted City Mayor of Leslie, just to sit back and let children draw houses in all those different colours of chalk on the pavements on the very street he lived..??... Oh no !!... On his patch ? ..

Children might get away with that kind of behaviour in other cities. .But not in Leslie...And most definitely not up the Bowery Quarter.. No way!!  Ever !!......Over his dead body..

So he'd told these would be Rebels.. Murderers and Rapists the tooth fairy wasn't real either....Then he'd stormed off in disgust, his walking stick Click..Click..Clicking...Beating out time on the pavement .

.''Click..Click..

''Click..Click''.

''Click..Click''

.''Click..Click''...''.

Cindy knew that clicking sound reminded her of something...?..She did..

Then she had remembered…. It sounded just exactly like Daddy when he was walking across the laminate flooring in his pink high heels..

When Daddy was teaching her to be a good girl.. With the Strawberry flavoured yoghurt.

Cindy liked it when Daddy was teaching her to be a good girl.. And the funny thing is. .Before Daddy had rescued her from the kennels. Cindy had never even tasted strawberry flavoured yoghurt before.. She'd never even heard of it ….But now.. She loved it.. Loved it. She couldn't get enough of it now..

.."*Just lick*" Daddy would tell her. "*.Just lick Cindy darlin'..Be careful and don't bite Daddy's sausage*" He would say gently…Then he'd tell her. "*.You're a good girl Cinderella…. A Good.. Good Girl.*".

"*Cindy*" Had also got her own revenge on these Hooligans…

Oh aye….She had indeed.. These Rebels needn't think they're getting away with behaving like that on Daddy's patch.

.So…"*Cindy*" had Shat on the pavement…Unseen by Daddy.. Of course. .Of course..

Oh "*Cindy*" had been very angry alright..

She knew fine Daddy would be very angry as well.. Because.. Just last year.. When she had her litter of eight puppies.. Daddy had been kind enough to invite all these children many times, in to see *"The Puppies"*..

Daddy had even offered to teach these visiting children how to play hide the sausage.. Or was it find the sausage..?. .

The ungrateful little Brats.. Chalking Houses on the pavement..??..On Daddy's patch as well. ???.... No respect these young ones nowadays.. None whatsoever....

So Cindy leaving a huge hot steaming turd lying on the pavement wasn't enough payback for these young renegades.....In Cindy's eyes anyway..

Thankfully ...It had started raining by the time she had her yoghurt.... And the rain had washed all the houses away.. Daddy had been so glad. .Because he was planning to go out with the bucket full of hot water and his sweeping brush to do exactly what the rain had done. *"The Lord Is On The Side Of The Righteous"* He'd told Cindy..."*The Lord's sent the rain to wash away the Devil's work Cinders"*.

And *"Cindy"*??. Well Cindy had barked three times in agreement.. She was thinking about getting even more strawberry flavoured yoghurt.

It was after this incident. .And in an effort to protect the other residents of the Bowery from such hideous crimes ever happening on their doorsteps again.. Ryan had formed the B.C.V.A.. ( *Bowery Citizens Volunteer Army* )..

He voted himself in as the Captain in Chief.... And despite Ryan's promise to arm all volunteers with Tazer Stun Guns in case the children might turn violent.... The appeal didn't recruit many volunteers .. ..Just the two.. Ryan and *''Cindy''*.

*''Aye well''* Ryan had told Cindy at the time. *''Aye well Cinders...On their own backs be It Darling.....On their own backs be it''*..

In fact.. The only reaction the Captain In Chief Of The Bowery Citizens Volunteer Army got to this appeal was that somebody?. .Somebody?. .Somebody chalked a massive big huge cock and an even bigger pair of balls outside his front door. ...In Blue chalk in case you're interested. .However the arrow pointing to Ryan's door was drawn in Red chalk..

Ryan had the crime scene all taped off and photographed long before the forces of Law And Order arrived..

Even *''Cindy''* had barked another twice at the audacity of the situation......

She'd had lots of strawberry flavoured Yoghurt the previous night. But she was always in the mood for more...Always...."*Good girl*" Daddy would tell her..."*Remember. .Just lick Cinderella sweetheart.... Jist lick darling. .Watch and not bite Daddy's sausage,*".. .Then Daddy's legs would start shaking and he would moan with pleasure *"OOhhhhh"* ..Daddy would Go...'''"OOhhhhh"*...

Then Daddy would always say *"Good Girl Cinderella. .Good.. Good Girl" ..'''*..

But still to this day.. And despite Ryan's most thorough investigations, The culprit who chalked the huge cock and the pair of balls hasn't been brought to justice...Ryan and Cindy both have their strong suspicions though. .Aye do they..

Unknown to Daddy though.. Cinderella had got her revenge for this act of savagery as well.. How had she sought that revenge?.. How do you think?.. Yep. .A great big hot steaming one. .Right on the very pavement where these Rebels had been drawing houses with chalk....Every colour of chalk under the sun. .And she's done it every day since..

So I'm sure you can fully understand how that particular rumour about the children hiring *"Grey Cloud"* had started... ?

They were just vicious rumours though…The truth was, the L.P.D  ( *Leslie Police Department* ) hadn't a clue. .There was no rhyme or reason as to why anybody.. Apart from the children, would want to assassinate a God fearing.. Church going. .Decent.. Honest pillar of the community like Ryan Boyle. Who prevents Tsunamis..

Nuclear wars.

 Or major plane crashes ever hitting Leslie by stopping young children.. Some as old as 7 from ever drawing houses with every single colour of chalk under the sun, on the pavements at the Bowery Quarter………

Anyway… In light of the assassination attempt, security was to be tripled for this year's parade.. ..

 The girls had spent hours upon hours.. For the past  2 days finding out all they could about their Holiday destination…They'd trawled the News pages of The *''Leslie Gazette''* And had read there had been 36 drive by shootings last year.  Seemingly.. That was 10% down on the previous year…

There had been 19 bank robberies' as well….That was down 3% on the previous year.

.Rapes. .Attempted  Murders and actual  Gang related Murders were all up by various percentages…..

And of course   Thanks to the City Mayors personal intervention.. There was no children drawing houses with different colours of chalk on the pavements up  the Bowery Quarter either…

Leslie sounded an exciting place indeed…..A lot more exciting than Hollywood at least…..Christ.. Hollywood was so quiet at nights nowadays that you could hear a three legged Fox farting from half a mile away…

And what made Leslie seem all the more exciting was when they'd looked up nightlife in Leslie website. .Or I should say websites….Because over fifteen pages came up….Everything to the 18 Casinos situated within the City limits, to the 70 nightclubs….

They could even take a trip on the ''*Bonnie Linda*''. The floating Nightclub….. It sailed from the Walkerton Quarter.. Right up the River Leven….Under the newly opened Auchmuir Bridge.. All the way up to Loch Leven and back…Every single night of the week..

They could maybe rent out a luxury Barge on the Lothrie burn and Chug..Chug..Chug. slowly all the way to the Holl Dam…Stopping off at many of the riverside pubs and restaurants if they so wished..?…..

There was also a good few lap Dancing clubs in and around Leslie…If they fancied staying longer than the planned 3 weeks.. Or even if the cash was running low..

They could always pick up some work in one of these clubs. .

They'd also read that. Lad-Zone were playing there comeback concert at the  Spiritual home of Leslie Hearts F.C.....The Quarry Park Belledrome. ..Lad-Zone were playing The Belladrome the weekend after the Saint Patricks celebrations..

Both Girls were big Lad-Zone fans.  Not half...They had all the Lad-Zone C.D,s  although nowadays.. They just downloaded any of the bands songs... The two Gals would ride every single wan oh the group...Given half a chance...Oh yeah...And they were broken hearted when the band had split up after various scandals about them had rocked the music world...

.Firstly....There had been the Knicker-Gate scandal.. When a young lady had accused a certain member of the band of stealing her knickers off her washing line.. This rumour had quickly been put to bed. .Because at the time the phantom knicker snatcher had been at work.. This certain member of the band had been in Germany... Away on a 36 date world tour .....

Then there had been the Cocaine –Gate scandal....

The less said about that the better though. But If you Google it you'll read all about it..   That scandal had started in Moscow. While the Band were on tour there...

When the Russian police had raided one of the bands Hotel suite...Conspiracy theorists still claimed it was the K.G.B who organised the whole sting...They reckoned it was them who organised the Cocaine and the Hookers.

The theorists claim the reason the K.G.B had sought revenge on anybody who was from Leslie. .Anybody at all.. Was that Leslie Hearts had hammered Moscow Dynamo 4-0 in just two weeks before Lad-Zones tour had started,. Seemingly most of the K.G.B hierarchy had an awful.. Awful lot of money riding on Moscow Dynamo to win. .. .As if eh  ?..As if minnows like Moscow Dynamo had half a chance against the famous team from Leslie. .That is a laugh....As if ??. .

But at least the raid proved the boys from the band weren't Buffties ..Because some folk said they were you know.....Some folk said they were Leslie's answer to Village People...Just because they pranced about the stage wearing black string vests... Tight leather shorts and black leather peaked caps... .

.But it was all an act and the Cocaine-Gate scandal had blew that rumour out the winndae...But the boys were back together now. .That was the main thing.......

The Gals had often gave their fanny's the thousand rubs ..Fantasising about what they would do with the boys in the Band......

Rita's favourite fantasy when she was in that sort of mood and thinking about the Guys from Lad- Zone was...She imagined this was her last day at school...She'd been walking home after school had finished. .Just walking home. .Minding her own business ..She'd been thrusting her tits out when the boys from the building sites or workmen's vans had been whistling and shouting at her...And obviously.. She'd dropped her schoolbag a good few times... Accidently.. On purpose   She'd bent over to pick it up......Just so the boys could have a quick look at her knickers...Then she'd stepped off the pavement. .Just one step and this great big black stretch Limousine with tinted black windows had nearly hit her. .Just missed her by inches. .Rita had stumbled back and tripped over the pavement.. She'd fell on her back.. With her legs wide open.. She'd been a wee bit dazed ..But the Limo had done the right thing and stopped...The next thing was... She heard was a door slamming shut...Then she heard somebody shouting in a rich Jamaican accent...They were shouting and telling her they were sorry and they didn't mean it... ..Rita had lifted her head just a wee..Wee bit.. Just to find out who was doing the shouting...Only to see this huge Rastafarian hunk leaning over her....This big black hunk was wearing a chauffeurs uniform with the dreadlocks sneaking out from beneath his chauffeurs hat...Sneaking all the way down his back.. And he's now asking Rita if she needed a doctor ?  Rita had swooned.

.Her head's back on the pavement ...She'd accidently opened her legs much further...By this time a lot of guys from the building site were gathering round for a good look... .Cars and lorries were also screeching to a halt...All desperate to see this schoolgirls knickers......That's what Rita liked to imagine anyway...The Randy Bastards.. That's what she liked to think...She had closed her eyes... .But this big Rasta. .He'd shouted to somebody else sitting in the Limo...

He's shouting for them to give him a hand and that they'll need to take this girl to the Hospital......

Then she'd heard car doors slamming shut...

Then she'd heard a Skattish accent telling her they were very sorry..

And the very sound of a Skattish accent always made her pussy moist in the first place..

Then she'd heard another Skattish accent...

They were asking if she would be O.K?....

Then another Skattish accent. .

This one was saying ''Aye.. Ah think we'll need tae take the poor lassie tae the Hoaspital''...

She'd opened her eyes...Only to see it was George Thompson. .The lead singer with Lad-Zone who was asking if she was O.K.?..

She'd closed her eyes and swooned again...

Her head hit the pavement once more and she had opened her legs as far as she could...

The boys had managed to lift her into the Limo. .But they never went near any Hospital ..No they went to Nirvana... Because, once the boys had found out she had just left school that very day...They'd ravished her. .She'd told them they could take her anywhere. And they did.....I'm sure you can imagine what happened next in Rita's fantasy...Aye I'll bet you can.....George Thompson and the bands lead guitarist.. Steven McNaught had spit roasted her first of all.

 She was wanking Rab Broon and Willie Loch off at the same time...

Then they'd all swapped about... She'd shagged every single one of the boys in the band..

Then she'd shagged the big Rastafarian chauffeur into the bargain. .

She liked to imagine his was the first black cock she'd ever had..

She liked to think it was so big she couldn't even get her lips round it.

You talk about Ebony and Ivory?

 She'd had the most awsome time.

All those big hard cocks all to herself……..

You talk about a Gal being showered in spunk ?...Gawd..

And sometimes when she was imagining all this. .She didn't even manage to get as far as a thousand rubs. .Sometimes she only got as far as 500 before her body started shaking, quivering and she'd let out a scream of delight……..

While Madge's favourite fantasy about the band involved a bit  Hanky Panky ..A right good spanky involving,  Whips. .Leather straps...Handcuffs. .And a pool table

They'd never seen the boys live before and thought they'd missed their chance when the band had split up...But the comeback concert fitted in just nicely with the Gals visit to Leslie. .Most of the 75.000 tickets had been sold. .But they'd managed to see a pair for sale on E.Bay for $1000 Dollars each... Three times the face value... Mind you.. With the seats being in The John Forrest Memorial Stand. .They were the best seats in the Beladrome.....They'd order the tickets soon...As for the price ?  Whoa. The price didn't matter a monkeys ... Because these two ladies would be loaded with cash   Loaded.. And they'd be hitting Leslie soon …Where they'd be spending every single God-Damn cent of that cash. .And also. .Also.. They'd both be getting the arses shagged off themselves intae the bargain….

When these two Gals hit Leslie…They Leslie boys wouldn't know what hit them.....Happy days indeed. .Mind you. .They knew that all the world's most beautiful woman stayed in Leslie….Movie stars and Models.. They knew they would be no match for the likes of Erin McNaught…. But still there would be plenty men to go round.. Aye plenty.. Anyway.. These Gals only planned to stay in Leslie for 3 weeks or so…They could love them and leave them…Leave all the Leslie boys broken hearted. .That had been Madge's attitude towards men for a wee while now.. Love them and leave them. .Fuck them and forget them!!!.  Whatever…The Leslie boys would never ever forget the time Madonna and Rita had been in their City….These Gals would make double sure of that…..

Another added attraction for the Gals when they hit Leslie was that Leslie Hearts were playing Barcelona on the Wednesday evening after the Lad-Zone concert…And Leslie Hearts were their fave soccer team .  Ever. They both sent away for the New Leslie Hearts soccer tops. Home and away….They both had Leslie Hearts calendars above their beds.. Every single year…And once more..

Thanks to the wonders of modern technology.. The Gals could watch every single one of the Leslie Hearts games. .Via a knock off Digi box. .Madge had acquired it from George Naylor funnily enough.....Sometimes they went to see a few local soccer teams...The likes of L.A. Galaxy.. But they were shite and only attracted no more than 50 of a crowd.. And most of them were relatives of the players..... Not that the Gals were really interested in soccer..... But they fairly enjoyed the sight of all these fit muscled young men running about in tight shorts...And the thought of seeing Leslie Hearts in action. Well ..That was almost as good as seeing Lad-Zone, and if you think the fantasies these Gals had about the guys from the band were perverted ? , then you should hear the ones they had about the Leslie Hearts team...There was more guys in the Soccer team than were in Lad-Zone wasn't there?. ..And as the calendars showed.. They were indeed all fit muscled young guys.. Every single one of them a proud Skatsman into the bargain...Fit as fiddles. .In fact... Madge was certain that if you looked at Septembers photo of the team in the Hot Tub.. Just after they had hammered Inter Milan 7-1 in last year's Championship Cup Final ...She was sure you could see some of their Baw Hairs through the bubbles. .But if you looked closely enough. .With a magnifying glass. You could see some of their Baw Hairs.. Not a lot. Maybe just a dozen or so.. But you could see them awright......

And just like millions of females worldwide....Both Madge and Rita wished it was them who were in the Hot Tub with the Leslie Hearts squad.. .They both wished that instead of the guys having their hands all over the Championship cup.. ..They wished the Guys had their hands all over their tits..

They'd both ride fuck out these guys.. Substitutes. .Craig Noble.. The Manager.. Them all. .And if the grounds-men were Skattish ..The Gals would put a shift intae them anaw.. . And they could bet these players could Ride aw fuckin' night. .That's what the Gals liked to think anyway...All these lovely big hard Skattish cocks all to themselves.. Yum.. Yum. .Oh yeah..

 These Gals loved the Skatsmen awright...Even better if they were wearing a Kilt...But then again.. What girl didn't love a Skatsman in a Kilt???..

Augusts photo in the Leslie Hearts calendar showed the squad just as they were boarding the plane as they jetted off to play Inter Milan. .And they were all dressed in kilts of the Leslie tartan... .If only these Skatsmen knew what the sight of them in a kilt done to A Gal...?   Knowing fine that there cock and there baws were swinging freely underneath the Kilt.....

Madge had told Rita that you knew what Clan a Skatsman belonged too.. Just by putting your hand up his Kilt...She said when you put your hand up there Kilt ..And you feel a Quarter pounder ?....Then You know he's a MacDonald!!! ...

Madge's favourite fantasy involving the Leslie Hearts squad was. .

She liked to imagine she had been out cycling one beautiful summers evening...She was wearing her pink Lycra cycling shorts and her matching pink crop top.. With her bare stomach showing. .She had got a wee bit lost and ended up on this tiny rocky country path. .It was downhill all the way. .For what seemed like miles.... She'd past a field full of Horses on the way down. One in particular.. A big stallion had a hard on. .It had.. She liked to fantasise the Stallions cock was hanging like a child's arm with an apple in it....Nearly touching the ground. But she would never talk about these fantasies with anybody.. Especially not you.. She's not even met you.....Doesn't even know your name. So she's not going to tell you anything like that...No way. .You'd have to cut her tongue out before she'd tell you anything like that. These fantasies were between her and her favourite big black vibrator...Anyway. .Anyway...When she reached the bottom of this rocky path, she was on the highway...She'd got off her bike. Gasping for breath.. And with her cycling over all these rocks and bumps, .She was feeling like the Gals feel after they had been horse riding. .Horny as fuck…Her fanny was throbbing….Throbbing worse than her teeth throbbed when she had the toothache.. Her wee pink thong was soaking... But there was no cock about….And I'm sure you can picture her in your own mind's eye.. Madonna….Gagging for her hole and looking around for a bush she could hide behind so as she could have a quick thousand rubs...When all of a sudden, this single decker coach had drew to a halt beside her.. The door of the coach had swished open.. And this big hunk was walking down the few stairs.. Madge's knees had nearly buckled .Her legs had nearly folded beneath her.. .Because the hunk was the Leslie Hearts striker,.. Robbie Graham ..And he was wearing a kilt in the Leslie tartan..…Robbie smiles and he says to her..Awright there doll? Can you show me the way tae Amarillo??.....But Madge was barely listening.. Her thoughts were on the bulge in Robbie's kilt…He repeated himself.. And Madge had replied. .Amarillo?.. Gee.. It's just along the road she'd said.. Then she'd asked ..

*"Sure. .I recognise your face Dude…Are you no' Robbie Graham who plays for Leslie Hearts".??...*

*"Ah sure am doll"*. Robbie had replied..

Then Madge had got all Girlie.. She'd shoved her tits right in Robbie's face.

*"Oh!"* Madge had told Robbie in her fantasy...*"You're my favourite soccer player ever. .I've even got your name on the back of my Leslie Hearts strip"*..

This was true...But Madge continued. .*"And my pal Rita"* she says. *"She's got Kyle Sweeney's name on the back oh her shirt anaw"*.. This was also true...At that Point Robbie had looked around and asked Madge where her pal was? But before she'd got a chance to answer, Robbie nodded at her bike and asked if her tyre was flat ?. .The next part of her fantasy. .She couldn't explain ..And she doesn't know what made her say what she'd said or do what she done...But she'd reached out ..She'd slipped her hand up Robbie's kilt.. She'd grabbed his Tadger and held on like a limpet....She'd smiled widely and told him that her tyre was hard. .But not as hard as his cock.. At this stage in her Fantasy... Madge had told big Robbie he was a true Graham. .There was more than a quarter pounder hanging there alright..."

*"No McDonalds for you here Big Boy.....Hmmm..Hmmm..Yum..Yum...*

She'd gladly accepted Robbie's kind invitation to come on board the coach and meet Kyle and the rest of the Leslie Hearts team .Sha Hoor sir. .She'd nearly collapsed altogether when she noticed they were all wearing kilts .. They were on their way to play a big game against Amarillo Wanderers...But they'd just played with her instead...What an absolutely awsome time they'd had...They had her squealing with delight.. You talk about soccer players scoring..?   .. The Leslie Hearts team had scored with Madonna in that particular fantasy allright..Yes Siree..  Every single fuckin' one of them   Then they called on the substitutes as well.  And she always wondered why Quinn Payne and Gaz Mullen were on the substitutes bench in the first place ?  Because they had made as good a job of spit roasting her as Johnnie and Kieran.. The Moran brothers and the other first team regulars....

She loved to think all these young athletic kilted Skatsmen had shagged her senseless for hours upon hours in every way imaginable.. Aye.. Even that way... .They'd made her feel like the dirty Hoor she was at heart. .Then when she'd had her own wicked way with them all.....And after she'd got dressed. .Well.. Partly dressed.. Because she'd gifted Big Robbie her wee pink thong to keep as a souvenir..... She would have loved to have kept a pair of Robbie's Boxers....But with him being a true Skattsman..He wasn't wearing anything under his kilt..Och well.. Not to worry.. It was only a Fantasy.....

But she loved to imagine the Leslie Hearts team had simply chucked her off the coach.. And after a while   And after she had got her breath back.. She happily cycled home.. Aye.  Happily.   And after she'd done the thousand

52

rubs imagining all this and was lying back.. Sweating....And well and truly satisfied...She liked to imagine that apart from the Leslie Hearts squad satisfying the aforementioned perverted fantasy...She liked to imagine it was because they were all shagging her that they missed the big game against Amarillo Wanderers.....

While Rita on the other hand..

She loved to imagine she could bring the Leslie Hearts calendar to life ..Oh Christ she would love that.. Especially Septembers photo .

She liked to imagine the squad had invited her into the hot tub with them. Aye. .She liked to imagine Kyle Sweeney had slipped his big hard Skattish cock into her from behind... In whatever hole he fancied ??  ..She loved to imagine she was wanking off Craig Noble and Ian Watson at the same time and the bubbles were splashing everywhere.... In this fantasy.. Sean Flett . .Big Gregor Somerville. Darren Faulkner and some of the other guys were all fighting over each other...Desperate to shove their cocks in her mouth first.... She had told them not to rush.. She'd told Big Gogs that if he was as good at riding as he was at Thai boxing ?..Then he was welcome to batter her about the ring anytime.. Anytime he fancied. .So he'd swapped places with Kyle. Oh Sha Hoor sir. .Big Gogs didnae half get rattled in aboot her ring...

Then they'd all took a shot. . Oh yeah.. They did indeed...Rita loved that particular fantasy .. Loved it. She loved to imagine she'd nearly choked on all their spunk....Showered in it she loved to imagine..

If only it could somehow come true...

They were going the very place to make dreams like that come true though. .Weren't they ?? Yep. .They'd be off to Leslie soon.. Who's to say the Gals wouldn't meet any of the Leslie Hearts players in real life while they were on their visit ..Eh ? They had seriously discussed taking the guided tour around the Quarry park Belladrome on the afternoon before the Barcelona game.....They had more chance of meeting the players then eh?. .Who knows? The Leslie Hearts players could haul them into the home dressing room and they could all have a quick shag before the big game.? . Stranger things have happened...You never know what's round the next corner Do you ??......

They would have to book their tickets for the game soon.. That way.. The ticket would be waiting on them at the ticket desk....

These Gals wouldn't be taking the gamble of not booking a ticket. No way.... They wouldn't be running about outside the Beladrome on the evening of the game looking desperately for a ticket.. Not with the chance of becoming victim to some ticket tout charging four or five times the face price....

Another thing about Leslie was. .It had the most sophisticated underground  system in the world....And thanks to the wonders of the latest Japanese technology.. The Bullet trains .You could scoot from one side of the City to the other in just over half an hour. ..The Gals thought this would be handy. .Because they might have to book a Hotel further out of town as they couldn't afford to stay in any of the Hotels on Leslie Boulevard itself.. Neither would they be able to afford any of the Hotels in and around the Quarry Park Belladrome either. Well.. They could afford it. .But their money wouldn't last long at all...

Take the world famous Station Hotel Spa And Country Club for example.. Situated at the bottom of the Boulevard near Central railway station....Every room except one cost £1.500 sterling a night to stay there...The other room named ''*The John Sutherland Suite*'' cost £2.500 a night...

With its 25 meter swimming pool.. State of the art gym. Sauna ,Steam room and Jacuzzi. All residents also had exclusive use of the Station Hotels own 18 hole golf course. But 4 nights at the Station and their money would be almost gone... While the two Gals had been researching all the places they could stay in and around

Leslie.. They had obviously checked out the Station Hotel website. .A beautiful Hotel indeed.. The new owners, Margaret and David Goldie had spent an absolute fortune on what was already a 5 star A.A listed Hotel. ..They had Union Jack bedspreads.. Union jack pillows. .Union Jack curtains and a framed photograph of Queen Elizabeth of Great Britain in every single one of the 364 En suite bedrooms...Some of the comments about the Station Hotel on Trip Advisor said it was the only place to stay while visiting Leslie. .Peter Robertson. Leader of the D.U.P ..(Democratic Unionist Party ) had been invited over from Ulster to open the Station after the refurbishment. .He described it a true Protestant palace....

The Clansman.. The Burns. .The Greenside, and all the other Hotels on the Boulevard had all received 5 star A.A. ratings as well and all offered the same wonderful facilities and were around the same price range.. So something further out of the City centre would have to suffice...Aye that would have to do. .And they'd just get the underground into the City.. . Nevertheless. .All these top Hotels would be booked out with folk going to the Lad-Zone concert and Leslie Hearts supporters from all around the world be booking up for the Barcelona game ..

They'd have to book accommodation soon though..

But who's to say they wouldn't get a click at the airport eh ?..

Who's to say they wouldn't meet some rich old Skattsman with one foot in the grave and more money than a horse could shite..... Let on to him that it's Tru Luv ..Pump the old guy full of Viagra...Ride the arse off him. .The next thing is. .As if by magic. You've moved into his Mansion. .Full Time.. You've got the number of his cashline card. You've also got your paws on his American Express gold and the rest of his credit cards.....

And he's making his True Love the main beneficiary to his will.. Happy days  ..Happy days indeed..

Who's to say things like that couldn't happen eh ? Wannabe Pop stars done it all the time. Look at her with the Massive Tits? ..''*Jordan*''..

And talking about pop stars...With *''Tin Pan Ally''* And many more recording studios situated in Leslie.. That meant all the famous rock stars were known to hang about Town...All the stars from the Movie world too.. Well.. With all these famous Movies being made in Leslie.. They would be hanging about town.. Wouldn't they..?. .I'm sure you know what the Gals fantasies were when they thought about getting a click with some famous Movie star when they were visiting Leslie..? Aye. .That's right. ..Fame and Fortune. On the Lorraine Kelly show and everything..... ...And if that did happen.? . They could stay in Leslie forevermore...They'd have plenty cash then.. They wouldn't need to grow weed for Barry Bang Bang any more..Naw.. They'd be out of Barry's clutches then.. Maybe ?

The two Gals had tried to guess what Hotel the Barcelona team would be staying at when they were playing Leslie Hearts.. .And I'm sure you know the thinking behind that eh ?..Aye.. They'd ride fuck out every one of the Barcelona team as well..?....

So that's that then.. You know the background to the story. .Now you know why the two Gals are sitting in Madonna's living room. .Trawling through the City of Leslie websites.. You know all about their planned trip to Leslie.. You know all about how they came to have the money to pay for the Holiday .With Madge winning all that cash on the scratch-card. .And you know about Rita getting a whack of cash from the miss sold P.P.I claim.. You also know all about the lovely cash that was coming their way next week.. When the weed they were growing for Barry Bang..Bang was dry...Then one of Barry's crazy sisters would be round to collect it. .And hopefully. .Hopefully ?... Hand over the cash...You also know about them drying some of that weed from Barry's crop in Madge's Microwave. .Not a lot though. .Maybe half an ounce between them. .But how much more of the weed would they have smoked by the time next week came eh ?..Aye.. That's a question you maybe never thought to ask yourself ??..By the way.. In the time it's taken to tell you this bit of the story. .They've had another two joints off that self- same weed...The Gals had obviously discussed the idea of just selling all the weed. .The lot.. Sell it on the cheap on the street. .They could make an absolute fortune. .Go to Leslie and never come home... Well. .If they sold all the weed.. They wouldn't be able to come back would they..??..But imagine the ready cash they could make?. .Even selling it at $50 a Quarter.. That's $200 an ounce....They each had 26 plants nearly dry.. Barry had said you get an average of 9 ounce from every plant.. If you do the sums. .It is a helluve lot of ready cash.. This idea was put to bed. .Very quickly...Oh yeah.. And I'm sure you know the reason why. .. .That's right. .Before they had even sold an ounce. .Barry bang  Bang would have heard all about it...And you know what happens next. .Don't you.?? Yeah. .That's right.... .Gee. .Wasn't  his sister Jean,  in the state penitentiary doing a 7 year sentence for trying to murder somebody who done just what the Gals were thinking about ??..Ideas like that are better off just staying ideas..

You know Madge and Rita's plans when the hit Leslie. .Yep...The woman of the City would have to lock up their sons. .And their Husbands too...You know about Madonna screaming and asking Rita if she would ride the Dude whose near naked. .Kilted Torso was staring out from her tablet screen. .Remember I was telling you about it at the very start of the story?...You know Rita had looked and gladly agreed that she would get her gums around that Dudes plumbs alright….. And I was just about to tell you who that Dude was. .I really was. .I was on the verge of telling you but Rita's Cell Phone chirped.. A Text message had arrived. She picked up her phone.. Checked who the message was from.?  .When she read it. .All she said was ..*"Aw fuck.. What is that moanin' faced Hoor wantin'"*?..She showed her phone to Madge...The Text message only contained 7 Letters and two kisses….. ***C.U. SOON..B.. XX***….  B was another friend of theirs....Well not so much of a friend nowadays as an acquaintance.. For instance. .She didn't know anything about the scams with the catalogues or Bright-House or anything like that...But it didn't take her long to twig on to the fact that both the Gals were growing weed in their attics... Because each time she'd been round visiting one or the other of the pair... Rita and Madonna had near hand went around the twist with the old Paranoia if they heard a car door slamming.   Absolutely convinced it was the Drug Squad coming to bust them. Or if a Helicopter flew over- head.. The Gals had jumped up and ran to the window.. They'd been convinced it had been *"A Bear In The Air"*..The Polis Helicopter….Out with the heart seeking equipment. .And if there was an unexpected loud Knock ..Knock. .Knock at the door ? .Gee.. The Gals had nearly shat themselves altogether. Thinking it was the man from the Electricity board come round to read the meter unexpectedly... .No siree..It didn't take Beyoncé Knowles long to figure out they were both growing weed in there attics....But it was turning out the only time they ever saw Beyoncé nowadays was when she was on the Mooch for one thing or another...

Be it Tea bags. .

A wee drop Milk.

A  couple of spoonfulls of sugar.

Twenty Dollars to see her through until her money from the Dole was in her bank account....

 But in reality. .All she really wanted was a free smoke of weed and some daft clown to sit and listen to all her problems.   And fair enough.. She always brought the stuff back. .Oh yeah,, But that was just another excuse to sit for hours and moan..Moan..Fuckin' moan.. The two Gals were sure Beyoncé was Manic Depressive.. Something along that spectrum anyway... Beyoncé tried to say that she was just highly strung.. Overly sensitive .. Being Emotional izznae a crime she used to say….. Aye. .Right.. She was a fuckin' fruitcake half the time…. P.M.T was terrified to go near her the other half. .And she thought it was cool to open up about her Mental Health difficulties any time she paid a visit.. She can go and take a flying fuck to herself……It's alright your pal pouring their heart out to you. .Now and again…Aye. .Now and again. Every single person needs a shoulder to cry on…But the Beyoncé one. She's just too much.. Because it's all the time. You should have seen the state she got herself in after Goldielocks.....Her pet Goldfish had pegged it…..She was up and down like a Yo-Yo for months…It's rumoured the Samaritans hung up on her that time.. And it's no other wonder..... But now Beyoncé knew they were growing weed.. The Gals didn't think they'd get a minutes peace from her…Mooch..Mooch..Fuckin' Mooch. .But naw..They hadn't seen her for the past fortnight …

''Ah thought she wiz away doon tae NooYoyk tae meet that artist Dude she'd met on plenty oh fish'' Madge asked…..

  "Artist "?..Rita replied. ''.The lyin' Hoor telt me he wiz a furniture maker an' a wood carver".

"Oh yeah''.. Madge agreed.. '''She telt me that anaw. Seemin'ly he's a musician tae.. Right talented Dude she says…Maybe loaded wi' cash.?  But it's a mystery how she'll see us soon…   If she's awa' doon tae Noo Yoyk'' ?

It was a mystery indeed.. Considering Noo Yoyk was days away by coach.. Aye. .Beyoncé had travelled all the way to Noo Yoyk by Greyhound coach…Paid her own fare and everything.... She'd told Madge that it didn't matter if she paid her own fare.... Because it might all be worth it. If only she could find a stable relationship.. She was looking for Tru Luv. .And of course you know Madonna's reply to that statement don't you?.. Aye ..She'd told Beyoncé she was round the fuckin' twist ...Tru Luv only exists in Fairy tales she'd said. .She'd told Beyoncé the only man who'll ever truly luv you is your Pappa..Mind you.. Her own Pappa had been a right one for preachin''..It didn't matter how much she told him not to. .He'd still be on and on..Preach..Preach..Fuckin'..Preach.. She'd never been so glad when she got word of her very own council flat...Away from under her Mamma And Pappa's feet...Him and his preachin''   And of course.. Having her own wee flat meant she didn't need to sneak men in and out through the Lavvie window...She didn't have to stay quiet when she was riding fuck out them...But as for the Beyoncé one. .Madge could just imagine her away down in Noo Yoyk City with the Artist. .Musician and Furniture maker.. She could just picture him.. Standing with a raging hard on. .Desperate for a right good shag.. And Her.. Beyoncé.. She's sitting with the tears blinding her..' ..Telling him she's not in the mood. .Because she's depressed. ..Still traumatised over the death of Goldielocks...The daft Hoor even had a funeral for the Goldfish.. She did. .In her back garden ..With the scented candles. .The dream catcher and everything .Josh sticks

63

the lot.. .But that was nearly two years ago. Sometimes when greeting about Goldielocks's demise.. Beyoncé would get all deep and meaningful about things and come away with shite like. …

.''The only way ah kin describe me an' Goldielock's relationship'' She would say..'' Is to compare it with a man's relationship wi' his dug.. She was my best friend ever…Ah could tell that Goldfish anything. Anything at all. Ah could even tell it where ah stashed ma secret stash of weed and everything…. .And I could be %100 certain she would not whisper a word to anybody''.. Then she would say. ''.And it's not many humans you could trust with that kind of information is it ?'…

.Tellin' ye' man.. That Beyonce wasn't all there in the head.. A few sandwiches short of a picnic.. If you know what I mean..??. A few paving stones short of a driveway….And sometimes when she was going on like this. .Madge used to think to herself…. Aye. Goldielocks might be ye'r best pal ever.. .But it's no' fuckin' Goldielocks that ye'r tappin' the Tea bags an' the sugar an' milk an' free smokes oh weed aff oh is it ya Hoor.??.

Sometimes Madge used to ask why Beyoncé just used her first name all the time ?...It wasn't as if her last name was Castle was it. .Beyoncé Castle? And Madge would laugh….

Rita broke Madges train of thought as she lit up that big Grass joint she was building and asked..

*"Dae ye' hink Beyoncé"ll be ridin' that Artist Dude Fi' Noo Yoyk ? Or dae ye' hink she"ll be sittin' greetin' aboot Goldielocks aw day"?*

*"Ah wiz jist hinkin' the very same thing"* Madge replied.. *"You musttovv been readin' ma mind again ya cow'.*

And Rita just smiled to herself... .Because the Gals were like that a lot nowadays.. They both had an uncanny way of knowing what the other was thinking. .Maybe it was spending too long in each other's company. ? .Gee.. Ever since Rita had moved across the landing,.. They were in and out each other's houses all the time. Who knows what it was ?..But it was uncanny. Even spooky sometimes....Almost a psychic connection you could say. .Take for instance the time .It was maybe 6 months ago ..When the Gas Engineer from the Council had come round to service Rita's boiler. .He'd swanned in and introduced himself as Rab. Rab Hood.. The two Gals had just looked at each other. .Not a single word was shared between them. .Not a word. .Just a look. .And that look told them all they needed to know. .That's right...The telepathic airwaves were telling them It wasn't only Rita's boiler that was getting serviced. ..They waited until Rab was finished work on the boiler then they'd both cowped him.. Just like that very first look had told the Gals exactly what would be happening….It was the very same story with Paul Quinn.. The window cleaner. ..Like I was saying Telepathy. .If they were lucky. .It would be an annual service they would be getting from Rab.. The Gas engineer .If not him.. The council would send somebody round to service the boiler.. And service these two council tenants into the bargain......

It was a fortnightly arrangement with Paul Quinn ..The window cleaner though..

*Rita reckoned she took this particular habit from her old English Granny.. It wasn't the window cleaner her Granny Ora was riding though. .Or maybe she was. .But never got caught,, It wasn't the council Gas engineer either ...Because the houses in London's East end didn't have gas heating at this time. All the houses only had coal for heating.. ..And that was the problem., .Rita's Granny had been caught riding..Johnie Lawson ..The coalman…. But her Granny had said up until she was caught. .It had been the perfect arrangement. .Just perfect ..Because Rita's Granny had got her coal for nothing.. While Johnie Lawson had got his Hole for nothing..*

*It was only then that Rita's Grand Pappy had twigged on as to why his wife had so much spare money to spend on Gin and the Bingo...*

*While Madonna ..She reckons she took it from her old Italian Gran. When Madge had just turned 16,..Her Italian*

*Gran gave her a bit of sound advice regarding men ..."*
*Men?"* Her Gran used to advise her in her Italian
accent... *'Men ?..They're a fine a for a scratch Madonna*
*hen.. ..So they are . Men are fine for a scratch .But then*
*again "* She used to say.." *Then again ..*"You're not itchy
all a the time". !!!* .

Another one of her Italian Gran's advice about men
were..."*You a mind a Madonna hen.. You a mind . When it*
*a comes to da men . It's Any Da port In Da Stoarm'''..*

Yeah ..Madge had kept her old Italian Gran's words of
wisdom in mind alright. .*"Any Da Port In Da Stoarm"*..
She was some case old Granny Carlioni..

Another piece of her old Granny's wisdom regarding
affairs of the heart Madge had kept in mind was. The best
way to get over a man. .Her old Granny used to say.. The
best way to get over a man Madge hen... Any man.. Was
to lie below another man as quick as possible..

By reading these stories.. You may be left thinking that
these two Gals are nothing but a couple of cock hungry
bitches. .And they are. They'd both be first to admit they
both loved their hole. .

But as Madge often pointed out to Rita. .Guys are just the
very same. They're every bit as bad when it comes to
getting a ride... She often used this particular scenario
when ranting on about men...

*''Imagine this''* She'd say..*'' Imagine a gang of about 4 or 5 guys ..Right ...And imagine this beautiful young woman passes them   A stunning looking woman.....She's got legs right up to her neck and she's wearing a braw pair of Red shag me shoes with four inch heels...She's wearing a skirt that's so short you could see her arse cheeks. .And her Titties are hinging' oot her low cut top for all to see...What dae you hink's the first thing to go through these guys mind eh ''?? Dae ye' hink they'll be hinkin..''That poor Gal must be frozen goin' aboot like that in this kind oh weather''?*

And Rita would always say..*''Naw''*

And Madge would ask her the question again. *''Well what's the first thing that*
crosses these guys minds when they see that beautiful Gal *wi' her Titties hingin' oot then''??*

*''Ah'd cowp it''* was always Rita's answer...

*''Exactly''* Madge would say.. *''Eck Fuckin' Zaktly.....Ah'd put a shift intae her'.....That's what these Mutha fuckers'll be thinkin..Every one oh the Mutha Fuckers... They're every bit as Bad as us Gals...If they're no' Gay like''..*

While Rita's favourite rant when the subject of Men came up.. Which was quite often ..But her favourite rant was about the P.C brigade. .She hated the Politically correct brigade with a vengeance. .She said they were all virgins ..She was certain the P.C brigade were all old folk who'd never had a ride in their entire lives.. Because what kind of a person would make up a law saying that a Guy couldn't wolf whistle at a Gal. Eh ?..Most Gals Rita knew were delighted if a Guy wolf whistled at them...Over the moon they were being admired.. Even Lesbians and Gay men liked to be admired by those of the same persuasion...It was getting to the stage with these Muthafuckers from the P.C. brigade that a guy couldn't even compliment a Gal. .Without them getting into trouble. . Take for instance the other day there. .When Rita had been going shopping and was just approaching the traffic lights...                    A Dude who was the passenger in a builders van had rolled down the window.....He had short  cropped blond hair ..Deep blue come to bed eyes. .His teeth were whiter than virgin snow. .He had that Scandinavian ....Viking look about him. .....Or maybe an Ex-Marine or Navy S.E.A. L......The first thing Rita had thought was  Sha Hoor sir.  .Ah'd ride him.... She was imagining his naked body entwined around hers.. .But the Dude had just winked and said.'' .*That's a lovely pair of titties you've got there Hun''* Then the lights had turned red and the van sped away,, .But did Rita run away and tell the Doctor she needed counselling because she was traumatised.. And felt sexually abused by this Guy's comment ?..Naw did she hell...If the van hadn't sped away from the traffic lights so fast, she would have thanked the Dude...Maybe slipped him her cell phone number ?.....Rita had been delighted... Absolutely delighted....Gawd..She'd put her wonderbra on special before leaving the house...And it was great to know that her efforts were appreciated... Every single Gal she knew liked the Guys to admire their Tittes....And just to think the P.C brigade would have that Dude on the sex offenders register......Rita was certain the frigid old folk at the P.C. brigade were trying their dambdest to take away peoples basic human instincts... Political correctness.. Gone right around the twist....When ranting on about this subject.. She liked to use Adam and Eve for an instance...She would ask if Eve said to Adam

*'Never mind trying to soften me up with apples Adam...'If you dinnae put your Bobby away... Ah'll get you done for indecent exposure...?? ..Do you think Eve said to Adam. .''If you put your haund anywhere near ma fluff Adam... .I'm telling the polis.. You'll get the jyle and you'll be on the sex offenders register fir the next 10 years''.?? Or even if you look at me the wrong way or even wolf whistle at me you'll get done fir bein' a sex pest.....*

Naw did Eve fuck say that...Everybody knows what Eve said...But If she had. .The P.C. brigade wouldn't even be here themselves.. So there......How the hell was a Gal ever going to get their Hole if Guys were scared to even look at them the wrong way?  ..Never mind talk to them. .Eh ?..That's the way Rita looked at things anyway.. Gawd there were times when Rita was sitting on a bus maybe. .Or in the Sauna or the steam room and if there was two or three Hunky guys sitting. .She just couldn't keep her mind off all the things she could be doing with them. .She described it as like a scene from the"*Oor Willie*" comic books. .When the devil is on one shoulder and he's shouting. .

*"Just grab them by the cock Rita .. Go on. .They're wanting you to Rita... Go on Rita.. Go on.. Get ye'r gums around their plums Rita"*

And the Angel would be sitting on her other shoulder. .Shouting .

*".No Rita.. You musn't ...No Rita don't...You're a Good Girl Rita,,, No. .Rita ..No..*

And the wee devil's shouting

*"Yeah Rita. .Just grab them by the cock.. Think of all that lovely fun you could have Rita. .Rita ...Ye'r a Hoor  .Ye'r a Hoor Rita"..*

And the Angel's shouting ...

*"No Rita. .No.. You like your Hole. .But you're not a Hoor.....If you as much as brush up against any of these Hunks. .Even though it's an accident. .They can phone the Polis on you Rita.. They could and get you done for inappropriate touching"..*

All that shite fair done Rita's head in...So it did. ..Gals liked their Hole.. And Guys liked their Hole.. End of.. What's all the problem about ??

*By the way.. You may have noticed the two Gals have been practicing their Skattish accents for the big adventure to Leslie.....But personally. .I think it sounds pish. Especially Rita's......I don't think it sounds Skattish at all...It's still got that annoying fake American twang about it... I mean Skattish folk don't use words like Dude or Guy ..Unless they've been watching "The Simpsons" too much...What dae ye' hink yersel??*

We'd better get back to the Gals conversation about Beyoncé though.. Because she'll be with us soon. .And I'm sure you'll want to hear what's being said..

They had discussed about what had went wrong with the Artist Dude fi' Noo Yoyk ?  ..And had went through all the scenarios about why Beyoncé was now on her way home ?..You'd have thought with her being away for a fortnight. .She would be having a great time. .Maybe she had found Tru Luv ?

Maybe she was bringing the Artist up to Hollywood with her to meet her pals..? But anyway. .You'd have thought she would have sent her pals a wee Text Eh ?.Maybe a wee Foatie or two.? .You know the kind of Foaties I mean.?.."

*"Here's a Foatie of me and my new boyfriend. The Woodcarver"* ..

*"Here's another foatie of what the luv of my life. .The Furniture maker made me for lunch."* .

*Or maybe...*

*"Here's a foatie of a painting my Hunnybun... The Artist done of me"* .

All that shite.. But no.. Nothing from Beyoncé. .Not even a Text to say the Artist had turned out to be a wanker. .Not a thing about the size of his whanger...Nothing.....A mystery indeed. .Ach well.. Like she says.. She'll see them soon.. They'll find out all about it soon...And Madge didn't think Beyoncé would really be the bearer of good news....

 It was Madge's turn to make something for them to eat today....The Chase was due on the telly soon.. And for normal. It didn't matter if it was Madge's house or Rita's... They'd have their Tea. Have a wee joint or two and settle down to see how many questions they could or couldn't answer. .

Not that they were competitive or anything like that. .Christ no.. They were the best of pals. .But they still loved to outdo each other. .Whether it be *''The Chase.. Pointless ''* or any of the other quiz programs that were on.. Gee. Sometimes the neighbours must wonder what was happening when they heard the two Gals shouting and swearing at the telly while these programmes were on.......If you're a fan of the above mentioned programmes ?.Then you'll know exactly the way they were shouting and swearing   .. And it was even worse when'' *Countdown''* or *''Who Wants To Be A Millionaire''* was on.. Mind you *''.Mastermind''* or *"University Challenge"* were a wee bit too much of a challenge for the Gals..

There was another thing they loved to tune into if they were up early enough and weren't watching *''Jeremy Kyle''*...A Skattish Radio station it was. .Oh aye.. They'd been searching for a Radio station that covers the Leslie area and stumbled across a Special station...Special indeed..

The Radio station was called *''Kingdom F.M''*…  And the Gals tuned into it thanks to the wonders of the Internet.. First thing in the morning was .*''The Breakfast Show''*.. Hosted by  Fife's Magic Mix... An Lovely couple. .Dave Connor and Vanessa Motion..

Both Madonna and Rita loved that show.. Oh Yeah !..

Apart from all the great Music and all the Hilarity and the Legendary Skattish patter….. It had a competition on it. .''The Word Is Out''. Where people phoned up and tried to guess what certain word was missing out of a sentence. .

It was a cash prize that went up every day….The two Gals loved to try and guess what the missing word was..?.. They never got it right though…Never..  To be honest. That competition drove the Gals round the twist with frustration. .It did.. And it seemed it drove all the Skattish listeners round the twist as well.. …It fair done their heeds in.. As they say in Skatland

And then…

At 10…

He's here again…

 Euan Notman..With his enchanted *''Mid-Morning Show.''*..

Euan had a part of his show called the *''Mystery Year''*.. Where he played music from a certain year in the past, and listeners phoned up trying to guess what that certain year was.?   . Oh Sha Hoor sir. .You should hear the Gals shouting at each other when Euan's *''Mystery Year''* was on.. …And sometimes they even got it right. .Sometimes…If they had phoned up.. They would have got a'' *Ding''* on the Dinger..

The main attraction for these two Gals though was of course. .Of course ..Dave and Euan's sexy Skattish accents...

Who's to say they wouldn't meet Dave and Euan while they were in Skattland eh ?..Who knows..??

If they did ? Apart from cowping the pair of them...They were going to sing them a wee song they had made up dedicated to their shows on *"Kingdom F.M."*. .They'd even wrote it in a Skattish accent an' awhing.....It's more of a poem at the minute really...Of course it would need a tune and another verse.. .But at the moment. It went..

*"We've wrote some words tae let ye' know..*
*We really truly love Ye'r show.*
*We love the Music that ye' play...*
*We love the competitions tae"..*

It was Rita who made most of these words up. .Although Madonna had more of an input with the chorus.. Which goes like this..

*"So both of us pledge our Devotion..*
*To these Guys and Vanessa Motion ..*
*We searched the Forth.. The Tay and them. .*
*But we love Kingdom. .Kingdom. .Kingdom F.M."..*

Then the second verse went..

*"We love ye'r accents and ye'r patter..*
*You're  miles away... But that don't matter.*
*Ye'z dinnae half cheer up oor life..*
*The uncrowned Queen and Kings oh Fife"..*       ...

Maybe the next verse would be about trying to get to the bottom of Dave Connors pockets..? ..And by Dave's own admission.. They are very deep.. Very deep indeed.. A true Fifer is how he describes himself...He loves a bargain..

But Vanessa Motion seemed to be a character of a Gal.. .Oh what..?  The uncrowned Queen of Fife indeed...What a fantastic sense of humour that Gal had..Awsome...And not only that.. She had a terrific lust for life as well...Absolutely Terrific.......

The Gal had just passed her Bus Driving Test and everything...

She even kept her own chickens that she'd rescued...

She's got her very own personal trainer at the Gym..

And now.. Vanessa's not long announced...She's got a piano she's learning to play...She's going to have her chickens dancing about the garden too some Richard Clayderman classic shortly.....

Now they've made up a song about Vanessa... Who's to say Vanessa wouldn't make up a tune to it ?..Knowing Vanessa.. This would be no problem....Maybe she'd play it on her piano?.. Maybe even have her chickens dancing about the garden to her own song ??..Maybe ??  ..

Who's to say Vanessa wouldn't turn out to be the Gals new .B.B.F..??..

They could maybe even see if Vanessa's interested in being introduced to Kunda Saharan ?

 If you have never heard of Kunda Saharan…  And if you are interested in finding out more about her ?   .Then I suggest you should read a book called *''CUNT''*  Yep.. That's the title. .*''CUNT*..

It's really easy to get your hands on a copy as it's available on Amazon…In fact.. You can check it out right away if you wish ?  .. Do you have your phone or Tablet handy ?..You do. That's great. .If you would care just to Google Amazon.. Then type in Des Dillon / Cunt.. ..Amongst all the reader's comments ..You'll see one comment in particular that  states *''Des Dillon's ''CUNT''. .Should be on more Bedside Cabinets than the Holy Bible''..* Can you see it..?.. Madge and Rita both agreed with that readers comment. ..Oh Yeah. .Oh Yeah indeed…It certainly was on their Bedside Cabinets.. Oh Sha Hoor Sir .Aye… If you like the reader's comments.. Then all you have to do now is press add to basket.. That's it….Then in a few days or so, you'll be the proud owner of one of the best books you could ever hope to read.. And if you buy another copy for your loved ones at home or abroad..?.. Then I can promise you.. They'll love you all the more for it.. They will indeed... Especially if you're loved one is in need of Sexual Emancipation...

Aye.. Maybe they could introduce Vanessa to Kunda Saharan...Who knows what's round the next corner ?

Remember I was telling you about these two Gals Telepathy ?..Well. .They'd both bought a copy of *"CUNT"* for each other as a Xmas present.. Imagine that Eh ?   It was the best thing they'd ever bought each other.. Wait until you read it yourself. .And you'll find out what they mean...

But I was telling you.. Madge had asked if they should wait a wee while and have their Tea later on.? .Because if Beyoncé got a sniff of the Italian dish Madge was making tonight. ? . She would hang about and Mooch some off them. .

The very mention of food brought on a terrible attack of the Munchies for Rita. .So she suggested Madge should just put the tea on now. .Beyoncé wouldn't hang about all that long anyway. .Once they started telling her all about their big holiday plans ...Oh yeah.. Beyoncé would be '' *Well.. Jell* '' when she heard about the two Gals big adventure to Skatland..... And she'd be green with envy when they told her it was Leslie.. The centre of the universe they were going to.. Leslie ..Fife..Skatland. ..The City that never sleeps. Whereas Hollywood..? Well. Hollywood is the town that never really woke up... And how they'd be painting that Goddamn town Red when they got there….Oh she'd be sick as a pig alright…. Because if anybody loved a Skatsman..It was Beyoncé…..

And there's her thinking she's the smart Hoor.. Away down to Noo-Yoyk..Looking for Tru Luv with the Artist and Musician.. ?..Ha.

If you've been paying attention.. You'll have noticed that Madge has been giving her living room a bit of a tidy up…A wee squirt of Mr Sheen here and there... You'll have seen her giving the living room carpet a wee Hoover. With the new Dyson so kindly donated by Brighthouse....

Beyoncé was a wee bit O.C.D about other people's tidiness as well you see….  And Madge didn't want her going about saying Madge was a clatty cow.    Beyoncé was guilty of carrying stories from one house to another. .Aye was she... .Oh aye.   Some folk said if you wanted everybody to know anything. .Just tell Beyoncé…While other folk. .They just told Beyoncé a lot of shite,. Because they knew fine she'd be away telling the story somewhere else. ...She's what Skattish folk would call A Gab..  Just like the Roving Reporter. .But you'll meet her later on..

The living room wasn't what you'd call dirty anyway....
More dusty.. With stoor from the local Quarry....Madge
was going to give things a quick wipe down later... But
that's her finished now....At this precise moment. .She's
just headed into the kitchen.. To empty the copper waste
paper bin...You'll have heard her shouting at Rita...In that
annoying American accent.. ."*Do you wanna cappa
Kaffee'''*"?...Rita accepted...So they had a cappa Kaffee.....A
cold sausage roll and another wee joint each... .Just to
pass the time for a while. And to satisfy the dreaded
Munchies until she made something real to eat.. Some
real Gal food. .The Italian dish she has in mind...She'd just
wait and make that later on...After that mooching' faced
Hoor  Beyoncé had shot the Craw...So while they do just
that..  .I could take a wee while and tell you about the
time the D.S.S thought they had caught Rita doing the
wee turn at the Lap Dancing club way down in Florida
Keys.. Remember I mentioned it earlier on?.  But wasn't
sure whether to tell you about it or not.. Well I'll tell you
now. Here's what happened.....The Gals would travel
down to Florida on the Friday afternoon.. They'd catch a
bit of shut eye on the coach...Even though they'd be
working until the Sunday night / Monday morning.. They'd
book into a cheap Hostel. .Just for the one night....In the
hope they'd get a click.. The click would of course invite
them to stay at their house wouldn't they?....Somewhere
to kip for the Gals.  .And there leg over into the

bargain...Braw.......They were making a right few Dollars.... They'd been working at this certain Lap Dancing club for just over a month .. When one Saturday night. .This stranger had appeared in the audience. .At first, Rita had thought he was a typical pervert...With the long cream coloured raincoat...The dark shades and the Baseball cap with the *''I LOVE LESLIE''* stitched on the front.. But the *''LOVE''* is in the shape of a heart....You're bound to have seen these kind of Baseball cap ??  ..Hold on though.. Hold on a minute...I'll have to stop telling you the story for a while.........

Can you hear the Thud.. Thud. .Thud of a Helicopter blades??...The two Gals certainly could....They looked at each other in a blind panic...The paintings on the walls are shaking.. Even the ashtray and the half full coffee cups were dancing about the coffee table with the vibrations....

Madge jumps up and was first to reach the window . .Followed very closely by Rita.. Madge dragged the net curtain aside, and you'll see for yourself... It was a Bear In The Air...The Polis with their heat seeking equipment. It's only just 20 feet above their house..... Thud. .Thud.. Thud. .Thud. .Thud...And it's dropping down.. The downdraft's blowing empty beer cans and plastic carrier bags everywhere.....It looks like it's getting ready to land to me... What do you think yourself?....

The Gals couldn't believe it.. Couldn't believe their fuckin' eyes….They were getting Bust…The Bears would find the tanks and the lights in the attic. .They would discover all that weed hanging up. .Nearly dry…  Nobody would believe 26 plants were for personal use. .Would they ?....They'd get done for dealing…And there is no way they could ever tell the Bears they were growing the weed for Barry..Bang..Bang. .No way.. Ever.......It would be years and years in the Penitentiary for them both. In beside Barry Bang.. Bangs crazy sister…And it wasn't Barry's fault they got Bust ..Was it ?..Naw..He'd lost all of his tanks. .His lights and most importantly. .The Bears had took his weed….But he would still want his Money…..What could they do?   ..They were Fucked. Well and truly Fucked…Then the Bears also would discover they had their Electricity meters rigged as well…They were fucked alright…O.M.G ..What were they going to do?...All their dreams of going to Skattland were up in the air now. They'd never get a passport now ..Not now they were convicted drug dealers…Everything had went Aw tae fuck.. All their dearest dreams had just new went pear shaped..

There was absolutely no point in them grabbing all the weed and throwing it out the kitchen window.. The Bears would have the place surrounded…

Madge's mind was already forming images of her . .In her prison cell. Scratching the Tally marks...Marking off the days.. Weeks.. Months and years on her cell wall...

While Rita?  She couldn't help but imagine some big. .Black She ..Male smiling widely at her...Like the big bad wolf smiled at little red riding hood..

The Helicopter's only about 10 feet of the ground now ..Just hovering there. .Waiting to land in the empty parking lot outside their homes.....

.It's Hovering ..Just like a Kestrel.. . .Can you see some of the neighbours are at their windows?  ...While others have rushed to their front doors.....And some of them are filming the whole drama on their cell phones...They'd all be wondering what the hell was going on ?....''A Helicopter landing outside the house'' ??..It's not every day you see that they'll be thinking...They wouldn't be long in finding out exactly what was going on though...

The Roving Reporter would be loving this.....Loving it.. Can you see her? . .Standing on her doorstep wearing her pink housecoat and even though the Helicopter's only, maybe 20 yards away.. She's holding her binoculars up to her eyes... .She'll be on the phone to that fat baldy clown of a son of hers soon...

*.The Roving Reporter had warned him though. .Aye..*
*Mummy had told him to stay well away from both Madge*

*and Rita...They'll get you into trouble she warned him...As if eh?. .As if..? You should see the state of him too.....But how he would love to ride the pair of them.. Aye would he....Because it'll be a good wee while since that man's had a decent ride .And of course.. You should see the Gals teasing him when they were sitting in the garden and he came on the scene in his big jeep. .With the personal number plate. .Thinking he's Archie.. But he's not kidding anybody.. Because it's all on credit. .The lot.. House. .Car.. Everything single thing on credit.. And in truth.... It's all show. .He's probably never had a day's happiness in his life...Not like these Gals. .Living the life of Reilly... But aye. ..You should hear the Gals laugh when they saw him standing..Perving...With his eyes almost popping out and his tongue nearly touching the floor when they were sunbathing in the garden. .Almost naked.... Then Mummy would shout on him..*

But that's who she'll be on the phone too very soon.... Telling him all the Goss.. All about Madge and Rita getting huckled out the house in handcuffs on and with blankets covering their heads.. Very soon .....The shame of it...It would be all over Facebook within the next few minutes...

There's the Roving Reporter put her binoculars down now.. They're hanging by a strap round her neck.... She's pulled her Cell phone from the pocket of her pink housecoat. .She's holding the phone up to her ear ..And you know fine who'll be calling don't you ? ...With the running commentary....She's ten times faster with the latest Goss than Facebook the Roving Reporter is...That's just one of her nicknames.. Other folk just call her Radar Lugs...She's like *"ISA"* In that hit Skattish comedy.. *'Still Game''* ...

Madge had rushed through to the kitchen.. She'd checked out the window.. She'd checked out the bedroom window as well...But couldn't see any Bears with guns standing on the rooftops or hiding behind hedges or that..??..

Maybe this Bust wasn't big enough to merit an armed S.W.A.T squad  ?   But there weren't even any police cars with the Blues and Twos shutting the street off..??  ...By the time she's back to the living room window.. The Helicopter blades had nearly stopped birling round...It won't be long now…...But here. !!!   Hold your horses.....Does that look like a Police Helicopter to you ??...It seems a bit small.. It doesn't look like it has heat seeking equipment or a Big Fuck Off searchlight on the front of it..??   ....It doesn't have'' *L.A.P.D.''* emblazoned across it either does it ?   .And there are no S.W.A.T teams jumping out the back of it ..The only thing at the back are some numbers and some letters.....Because it's only a two seat Helicopter. More like a private Helicopter than the Fuzz.

And it's not the Air Ambulance either..

*This fact alone would leave the Roving Reporter feeling rather disappointed though.. Because she loves a good accident so she does. .The more folk dead the better. She's holding her cell phone up to her ear with one hand now. .And is holding her binoculars up to her eyes with the other hand .I'm sure you can imagine the conversation she's having eh ?..*

And by this time.. You'll be thinking just exactly what the two Gals are thinking....Maybe you've even tuned into their Telepathy..?   ...Because they're both thinking.. Just what the hell's going on ?...

Rita was just thinking that the Helicopter pilot must have had to make an emergency landing.. When Madge interrupts her train of thought... ".*It's probably had to make an Emergency landing*" She says..... Rita. .She tells Madge that she's been reading her mind again...What did I tell you about their telepathy eh ?....

They both smile at each other. .Both thinking exactly the same thing again. .And that was.....Maybe the pilot's a rich young Hunk?...And if he's had to make an Emergency landing in his own Helicopter ?..That would mean he'd be loaded with cash.

He might be in a wee bit of distress eh ?....

Maybe the Gals could invite him up for a cup of tea.. Or something stronger??...Just to calm the poor boys nerves ? ...

Maybe a wee joint of weed ?  .Any excuse to get the rich young Hunk in their house .Then you know what comes next. .Don't you??...Yes  siree. The rich young Hunky pilot maybe wouldn't be in such a hurry to make an E mergency take off, if these couple of hot. .Horny bitches had cowped him...

.But the Helicopter blades have stopped birling now.. Even the wee blades at the end of the tail have stopped. It must be somebody making an emergency landing right enough.. How long do you think the Helicopter's been sitting there for now?   A minute ?..Two minutes ?  Oh wait.. Hang on.. .There's the passenger door opening a wee bit. .Then it opens a bit further….It's swung right open now...There's a woman looking out.. Can you recognise her?. The two Gals certainly could..Sha Hoor Sir.. It's her..   Beyoncé .It is.!!   It's fuckin' Beyoncé...She must have found Tru Luv right enough.  That Artist Dude must be loaded….Beyoncé takes off her shades ..She waves up to Madge and Rita. .They wave back...Then she starts waving to all the neighbours. .The show off. .She loves all the attention that Hoor .The Gals weren't jealous though.. Oh no...The Neighbours are all waving back...And by this time.. I'm sure I don't have to explain about the state "The Roving Reporter" has worked herself into....Can you see her ??

The two gals were both thinking that the Beyoncé one must be inviting the pilot up to meet her very best pals.. I mean. .What's a tea bag. ? .Or some sugar or a free smoke of weed amongst your best pals eh ?..Nothing wrong with that. .Nothing at all...Twenty dollars now and again until the money from the Dole goes into your bank account's nothing either. .It's the least you could do to help your bestest pal out.. And wasn't Beyoncé these two Gals very bestest pals in the whole wide world? Of course she was....Gawd. It didn't even matter if she shagged their boyfriends.. Oh no. Sharing is caring...It's no loss what your best pal gets......And Beyoncé also knew she was always welcome to pour her heart out to her best pals anytime she wanted...It didn't matter what her particular problem was...She was always welcome. .Anytime. And it wasn't Beyoncé's fault that she was highly strung...It was a shame for the Gal.. That's what it was. .An awful,. .Awful shame...A terrible shame.. These two Gals were good listeners though... .Oh yeah.. Especially now that Beyoncé had got in tow with somebody who had their own Helicopter. .The Jammy Hoor..

Beyoncé. .She climbs down the few steps.. She reaches up and grabs a few bags...The kind of bags you get from posh clothes shops.. The kind of bags with the string for handles…Then the passenger door swings shut. .It must have been pulled shut from inside…It would be The Artist ..Being a Gentleman…They'd find out what he looked like shortly..Sha Hoor Sir. .It didn't matter what he looked like. .Did it ?..Did it fuck…Hopefully…. He'd a cock to match the size of his wallet ??  Yum..Yum…. And they'd be getting introduced to him soon…They'd find out if they'd cowp him soon….

Beyoncé starts walking across to their block..
Madge. She runs to unlock her front door.. .Ready to offer the very warmest of Hollywood welcomes to her best pal and her brand new boyfriend. The Artist. .Who's loaded with cash.. Got his own Helicopter and everything…
She did have a quick thought that maybe she should run down the two flights of stairs and help Beyoncé.. Her very best pal.. Up the stairs with her bags.. The bags with the string for handles. .Like they were from posh clothes shops.?...And not just that.. She'd be first to get introduced to Beyoncé's new boyfriend wouldn't she ? And you know what that means eh ?...She's just unlocked the second lock when she hears a noise. .It sounds like the Helicopter starting up again.. She opens the door, rushes back along the lobby and looks out the living room window….Sure enough.. The Helicopter blades are birling away .

Madge just stares at Rita. .

Rita stares right back..

They both gaze out the window again...Beyoncé is
standing waving goodbye to the pilot...The Helicopter
lifts about 10 or 15 feet up in the air now. It tilts its
nose upwards...It reaches the height of Madge's second
floor flat window... Can you hear it ?  What a fuckin'
noise... .And then it's off. Away up in the air.. Away
over the rooftops.. Leaving the peculiar sound of
quietness..
Both the Gals were speechless....

The Roving Reporter .She's still gawping through her
binoculars.. Even though the Helicopter's no more than
a dot in the sky now....She's still gabbing away on her
cell phone too...Gab..Gab..Gab.. The Jungle Drums
would fairly be beating today anyway...I'm sure you can
imagine the conversation she's having with her son.
...Fatso would be dying to ask if Madonna and Rita were
both out watching Beyoncé getting out the Helicopter
as well..??..He wouldn't ask Mummy that though. .He's
been well warned. .Well warned..

But the Mystery deepens even further........

I know fine you'll be thinking exactly what Madonna and
    Rita are thinking.  But you'll get all your questions
    answered shortly... Because Beyoncé had just pressed
    the buzzer on the main door to the block of flats..
    Madge.. She nips back along the lobby.. She presses the
    button on the wall that would let Beyoncé through the
    main door.. Remember.. Madge's front door's still wide
    open.. Wide open to welcome Beyoncé's latest man..
    But that's not happening now is it.? .Not now that the
    Dude's away in his Helicopter.

## CHAPTER 3

## HERE COMES BEYONCE

Can you hear the main door slamming shut and the sound
    of Beyoncé's high heels click.. Click. .Clicking as she
    makes her way up the two flights of stairs.?  ..But
    Madge is thinking... Maybe the Helicopter pilot's away
    to refuel or something?  Maybe he'll be back soon.?
    Maybe be best to keep on Beyoncé's good side?.. So
    with that thought in mind she goes and helps Beyoncé
    up the last few stairs with her bags.. Madge notices the
    Hoor's dressed up like something off the front pages of
    "Hello" magazine. .She's also got a big M.K. handbag
    slung over her shoulder...She never had that when she

left for Noo Yoyk..To meet the Artist. .He must be loaded..Fuckin' loaded.. All the other bags she was carrying were from Harvey Nix. House of Fraser etc Etc...

Madge asks Beyoncé why she didn't invite her new boyfriend up to meet her two bestest pals in the whole wide world before he took off in his Helicopter ?.

Beyoncé just laughed and told Madge she bet her and Rita both thought it was the Polis when they first saw the Helicopter.

*"Aye fuckin' right we did"*...Madge replied In a Skattish accent.. Then she told Beyoncé all the things I've not long told you about a wee while ago. .All the scenarios that go on inside your head when you're sparkled with the weed and think it's the bears coming in a Helicopter to bust you....Then.. Once again.. She asks why Beyoncé hadn't invited her new boyfriend up. .For a cup of coffee or that?..

No way, Beyoncé thought...She knew fine what *"Or That "* means... There's no way she would be bringing this latest click back to meet these couple of Hoors..No chance.. She could just imagine the pair of them... Sitting flashing their knickers to the boy...They'd be bending over in front of him ..So as he could see up their skirts or down their tits.. She'd seen the pair of them in action with the Roving Reporters son.. They

93

weren't even getting the chance to tease the fuck out of this latest boyfriend......And if Beyoncé went for a pish or something. .These pair would quickly try and cowp the boy . .Aye would they...And Beyoncé had to admit.   .She'd shagged their boyfriends in the past.. .Madge and Rita had both shagged her boyfriends as well.. Sharing is caring...It's no loss what a friend gets. .And all that.. But the pair of Hoors weren't getting their paws on this latest boyfriend ..No fuckin' chance...Wait until she told them exactly who it was though. They'd be sick. .Sick they would be .As sick as somebody who's been nabbed by the Dole for working on the side.. They'd be Well..Jell when they found out who the Beyoncé one was riding now....

So instead, Beyoncé replies the Helicopter pilot was only her new boyfriend's personal chauffeur. That was all Beyoncé said. .....Leaving a silence that she knew Madge would fill...And as Madge back-heels her front door shut,  she was going to ask Beyoncé where her new boyfriend was.? ..But she thought she should show a wee bit of concern at least. .She was also desperate to find out what kind of new clothes were in the bags. .If she had been walking behind Beyoncé.. She would have managed a quick look. .Just even to see the price tags. .But you don't want your pal to catch you doing things like that. .Do you ?. So she tells Beyoncé that she hopes that everything's still O.K. between the Artist and her….Beyoncé tells Madge that the Helicopter had nothing to do with the Artist….It had to do with her latest boyfriend…But.. Nothing at all to do with the Artist……I'm sure you know what Madge is thinking eh?.. Aye. Trying to get information out this Beyoncé one was sometimes like trying to solve the Times crossword…..Anyway. .They're back in the living room now.. Madge drops the bags she was carrying. .Still not managing to get a right good look in them. .Yet…. And Rita.. Who was building yet another Grass joint and had caught the conversation.. She tells Beyoncé not to talk in fuckin' riddles.. A wee clue here and there …The two Gals had been most concerned for Beyoncé's welfare…. Away down to Noo Yoyk on her very own…*And Madge agrees*…..

Away to meet a Dude she'd never met before…A.W.O.L for a whole fortnight…And she had never even sent her best pals a text or fuck all. .They had been worried sick about her…..*And Madge agrees*…

They were even thinking about reporting her missing….*And Madge agrees*…

So the least Beyoncé could fuckin' well do was tell her best pals all the Goss. .*And Madge agrees*…..

What about the Artist Rita asks..?…And as Beyoncé flops herself down on Madge's couch.. She kicks her high heels off and replies that it was bad news and good news as far as the Artist was concerned…Bad news and good news??......Rita...She tells Beyoncé that she'd better give them the bad news first...*And Madge agrees* ..Give us the bad news first. .Cause the two Gals had good news for Beyoncé as well. .Didn't they.?? .Didn't they half...They'd be away over to Leslie soon wouldn't they?. .Leslie Fife Skatland...The pair of them would be living on the wild side of life when they hit Leslie..Fuckin' right they would. .And with all that lovely cash to spend into the bargain. .Aye.. Just wait until they told Beyoncé that.. And here's her thinking she's the smart alek, getting her new boyfriend's personal chauffeur to drop her off right in front of their houses in a Helicopter eh ? .... .She'd just done that to rub the two Gals noses in it.. That was all...Aye well.. None of these two Gals would admit to being jealous of the Hoor..In fact. .It would be Beyoncé who would be green with jealousy when they told her all about the forthcoming holiday.. Leslie. .Here We Come !!! .British Airways....First class....Away to see Lad-Zone and Leslie Hearts.. She Hoor Sir.. She'd be sick as a pig when they told her there good news....Because nobody loved a Skatsman more than Beyoncé........So...Beyoncé ..She takes her shades off.. She puts them in her big M.K. handbag.. She then pulls out a huge bag of weed. .A Fuckin' huge bag of weed......Madge thought there must be over an ounce in there...And Rita.? .Well you already know Rita would be thinking the exact same thing as Madge...Well over an ounce....And in between building a

96

big grass joint.. Beyoncé tells them the bad news about the Artist...

He'd met her off the coach in Noo Yoyk as promised..

Her first thought had been to look at the size of the bulge in the Dudes troozzers...

*"Wid ye' cowp Um"?*  Rita asks..

*"Well aye"* Beyoncé replies. *.."Cause he looked tae hiv no a bad sized cock ontae um like ken?"..*

*".Hmmm Hmmm"* Rita purred..

"Yum Yum" Purred Madge.. "An' did ye' cowp um"??

Beyoncé tells them she thought she was going to.. But she'll tell them more about that in a wee while...Then she says her second thought about the Artist was the photo he'd put up on his P.O.F. profile must have been about 10 or maybe 15 years old...

*"Bad sign babe"* Madge commented.."*Jist speakin' fi' personal experience like ken* ?..Even though Madge had no time for P.O.F.. Hadn't she warned them all about the dangers?. .But it was bad news concerning the Artist though. .And Madge couldn't wait to hear that bad news...Not that she was jealous of that Beyoncé Hoor getting dropped off in a Helicopter. .Oh no

..Madge wasn't jealous ..It was just that...Well. .You know fine well how Gals get with their best pals..??

*''Fuckin' right it wiz a bad sign''* Beyoncé agrees....Then she explained... She hadn't travelled all this way for nothing had she ? .. She was looking for Tru- Luv wasn't she ?..

Rita asks what age he really was? ..And when Beyoncé tells her he turned out to be nearly 50..Madge burst out laughing..'' *Nearly 50* "she guffawed. .*''Ye' wir gawn tae shag somebody who wiz nearly 50''?..*

Beyoncé told her to shut her puss and reminded her that she was 60...Wasn't she?  And she still wanted guys to ride her. .Didn't  she.?  Aye did she…. Even though she'd got her bus pass. .She still wanted guys to ride her...And as often as heavenly possible..
…
Madge did shut her puss . .In fact she changed the subject altogether by asking if the Artist had treated her to the slap up meal as he had promised...?
Beyoncé tells them he did indeed..

*''Where did he take ye? ''* Rita asks.

*"The Noo Yoyk Hilton"* Madge says jokingly. .Aye..
.Jokingly.. .Secretly she was hoping it wasn't true..
Cause that would mean the Artist was truly loaded. .But
it was bad news concerning him. .Wasn't it ?..It wasn't
his Helicopter was it?

*"Naw  Did he fuck take me tae the Noo Yoyk Hilton"*
Beyoncé snapped. ."He *took me tae MacDonalds"*

*"Mac Donalds"* ??   Rita chocked on the joint as she
laughed..  *"Mick Fuckin' Donalds.???..*

*"Another bad sign doll"* Madge told Beyoncé wisely
....."Any decent man lookin' fir Tru -Luv wid at least
take ye' tae K.F.C. eh* ?  And she laughed every bit as
loud as Rita was laughing.

And Rita passed the joint over Madge...

Beyoncé just looked at the pair of them.. She was
wondering why the hell they were trying to talk in a
Skattish accent?..

Madge has a good few sooks on the joint.

But then again.. Madge and Rita were both wondering
why the hell Beyoncé was trying to talk in a Skattish

99

accent?.. None of them knew what the other knew though.. Did they?..

Madge laughs. .She hands the joint back to Rita and tells Beyoncé once more that any decent man lookin' fir Tru –Luv would at least take his new found doll tae K.F.C…She'd also noticed there was no sign of Beyoncé's O.C.D today ..She wasn't rearranging the coasters on the coffee table…Nor was she rubbing her finger over the furniture.. Checking for the least wee bit of stoor.. She didn't check to see if the pictures on the wall were straight either..

Beyoncé. She lights up her own joint and takes a huge sook.....She knew the reason Madge was coming away with these smart comments….  She was jealous. .That's what she was....Fuckin' jealous ..And it reeked out her…Just because she was a washed up auld Hoor..Who'd not long received her bus pass…And Beyoncé had bigger tits than her too. Much bigger…And a longer pair of legs.. And a better looking ass. .Aye.. Well….Just wait until Madge heard who was riding that sweet old ass now…She would be jealous alright. .Just wait till Madge found out who'd been rubbing their hands up and down Beyoncé's lovely long legs and all over those big juicy tits …  If only the Madge one knew where Beyoncé really had been dining for this past two weeks…She'd be laughing on the other side of that Bo-Toxed face of hers...K.F.C ??    Ha  .If Madge only knew..???.....If only??..Still ....Madge was loving the bad news. .And if that's what she wanted?. .Then ...

So Beyoncé just has another huge souk at her grass joint... Then continued with the bad news... She told them about how the Artist. .Robbie... Robbie Villiers. .Had invited her back to his apartment... That turned out to be a bottom floor bedsit in the Bronx district of No Yoyk,..

A cowp of a place in the worst district in Noo –Yoyk...

As all bedsits are. .It was a bedroom come living room ...Single bed....And a tiny wee kitchen. .Painted black...No carpets on the floor or nothing. .The floorboards had all been painted jet black......

She told them about how there was no sign of the furniture Robbie ..The furniture maker...Had made himself...In fact ..What little furniture there was in his bedsit was from IKEA...

There was no sign of any musical instruments lying about either..?.. Not like a lot of guys houses she had visited.. A lot of them who professed to be musicians at least had a guitar or a Banjo lying about and gave the excuse of the strings being broken for not being able to give her a wee tune. .Serenade her before she cowped them……

It had taken her a wee while to catch onto that particular story……

Not that she was ever interested if any of these guys could play any musical instrument or not…As long as he could make her pussy lips sing.. That's all that truly mattered….But not a thing lying about Robbie's bedsit..

There was no sign of any paintbrushes lying around except the big four inch one that Robbie had used to paint the doors in his Apartment.

He had painted them all jet black….

The skirting boards.. The roof and all the walls were all painted black as well.. Except for the white skull and crossbones with a dagger through its head that was painted on the wall above the 12 inch portable television. .Which was sitting on an old oak effect IKEA unit….

Robbie had told Beyoncé that he'd painted the skull and Crossbones himself.. ..He'd described it as his *"Unfinished Masterpiece"*..??

He had an old video player rigged up and lying on the floor…She had noticed some of the videos.. The Texas chain saw massacre had been one of them..   The Hills have eyes was another..

It was becoming crystal clear to Beyoncé that she wouldn't be finding Tru-Luv with the Robbie one....Crystal clear.....But. .There might still be the chance of a quick ride..

Apart from the Skull and Crossbones. .There had been no sign of any of Robbie's own paintings hanging on the walls..... The only paintings were three or four Jack Vettriano prints. ...

And one of Jesus Christ situated above Robbie's 3 bar electric fire...

Robbie had told her the photo of Jesus Christ was actually Robbie himself in his younger days...

That's when the alarm bells had really started ringing with Beyoncé... Oh yeah.....The red flags were all up....Still.. There was always the chance of a quick ride though..

The only sign of any woodcarvings were three African face masks hanging on the wall....Robbie said he carved them himself when he was going through his *"African Art"* phase....

But when he'd went for a pish. .Beyoncé had checked on the back of the masks. .

One was made in Taiwan...

The other two were made in China....

That's when Beyoncé started thinking that it was about
   time she got herself to fuck…But. .If she wasn't going to
   find Tru-Luv ?  She wasn't travelling all this way and not
   even getting her hole..

Things had just went from bad to worse from there on
   in…Because Robbie's P.O.F. profile said he didn't drink
   at all…And this had been a big attraction for Beyoncé at
   the time.. ….
But the reason for him not drinking, was he was a
   reformed alcoholic…
He'd actually attended an A.A. meeting before meeting
   Beyoncé off the coach…..
So,….

With all this in mind. .They'd shared a few bottles of
   Buckfast tonic wine…Half a bottle of bourbon and a few
   grass joints…It was becoming crystal clear that Robbie
   was more a piss Artist than anything else.. But…Just
   when Beyoncé thought she was going to rip the
   knickers off him.
.Just when Beyoncé was hoping that Buckfast really does
   make you Fuck-Fast……Robbie had pished himself..
   Yep.. Pished himself.. All down the front of his tight
   white charity shop jeans…. That was just a few seconds
   before he was sick all over the top of Beyoncé ….Aye.
   .Sick as a pig he'd been…. Then he'd collapsed on his

bedsit floor...Unconscious...Then he'd let out a massive
thunderous fart.. Then there had been an awful smell
of shite. .It was obvious what happened.. Robbie's
bedsit had been reeking of it..

And how Madonna and Rita had both laughed at that.
.Laughed at what they thought was Beyoncé's downfall.
.And this is the Madonna and Rita .. Who. .Only 10
minutes beforehand, had been professing to be so
worried about Beyoncé being away to Noo Yoyk in the
first place..... Going to phone the police and report
Beyoncé missing because they hadn't heard a cheep
from her in a fortnight... They're full of shite,.. The pair
of them. .Full of shite...The only reason they're being so
concerned now. .Is because ..They're wanting all the
Goss.. And they're wanting right in aboot it..
Desperate to find out all about the Helicopter. .Thinking
maybe there's something in it for themselves..

But it's no wonder Beyoncé hadn't been in touch ..No
bloody wonder.......She was having plenty action.. She
was having a whale of a time. ..A ball....Neither of these
pair of Hoors knew this yet. .Did they ?...

But just wait until Beyoncé told them though.  .Just wait..

But they wanted the bad news first... So that's what
they'd get.. Just wait though. Just wait..

.And so.. She went on to tell them about how after that
carry on.. She'd took the scunner altogether. All this
way and not even a shag.. *''Fuck this''* she'd thought to

105

herself...She'd had a wash.. Changed out of her shag
me clothes. .Then she'd just grabbed her rucksack and
fucked off...

This had been about 10'o' clock on a dark Noo Yoyk night.
.

She told them she'd just walked and walked and walked
for hours upon hours. .

She also noticed none of the pair of them asked if she was
scared walking around the streets of Noo Yoyk on her
own?. Especially the Bronx...If they had asked ..She
would have told them the truth. .She'd been
terrified...But no. .Not one of them did ask... That just
shows how concerned they were for Beyoncé's welfare
eh ?..Aye. .It just shows you....


Madge and Rita just looked at each other as Beyoncé told
them about how she'd walked until she'd came to what
she thought was the sea.. But actually turned out to be
a river.....

They were both thinking that if this was any other story..
Then Beyoncé would be greeting her eyes out by this
time. .She would be.. The tears would be blinding
her..Gawd..Look how traumatised she'd been over the
death of Goldielocks. Her pet Goldfish. The Goldfish she
had a spiritual connection with...The mad Hoor....But
when it came to affairs of the heart. .She was 10 times
worse.. You couldn't keep her going in Kleenex tissues

when it came to affairs of the heart. But she was taking all this bad news very calmly ..Very calmly indeed....

.And that's not like that dirty stop-oot....

Beyoncé told them how she'd sat on some rocks on the sea shore for hours upon end ..It was maybe on the dock of the bay she'd been sitting ?..Just listening to the waves gently roll in.. And then roll out again... She'd sat there right until the Noo Yoyk blackbirds hid started singing... A bootiful Noo yoyk morning it had been...The Empire state building was about a mile or so from where she had been sitting.....Clothed in golden sunshine it had been......

She'd been sitting thinking about just flinging herself in the water loads of times throughout these long lonely hours...She'd been signing all the sad songs. .She'd been singing. *"Nobodies child"*. Remember that old Jim Reeves classic? *"Nobody wants me. .I'm nobodies child"* ..She'd been singing that R.E.M hit as well...*"Everybody hurts sometime"*.. But aye.. She'd felt like Just walking right in the water and droonin' herself to death.

 In beside Goldie-Locks in her spiritual home.....

And then.

All of a sudden..

She'd heard singing.. And it wasn't her echo...Was it fuck her echo.....Beyoncé hesitated ... .Leaving that pregnant silence again.. That pregnant silence she knew fine Madonna would be desperate to fill.

But it was Rita who filled it..

107

*"Singing"* ? Rita asked" *What kind oh singin'"* ?

*"It would be the blackbirds ye; heard"* Madge commented.

*"Naw Naw..It wizznae the blackbirds ah heard singin'"* Beyoncé assured them.. *"It wizznae the blackbirds .. The Blackbirds could only dream about being able to sing a song as sweet or as beautiful as this song....It wiz humans!!. .Men.!!. And they were singin' a lovely song they'd often heard many **a** homesick Skatsman singin'..*

Then that wiz when the bad news ended....

Both the Gals had noticed the Beyoncé one was still practicing her Skattish accent...A wee Skattish word slipped in noo an' again. .Like flingin' and droonin' an' that ken ?.

You'll likely have noticed yersel' that she's been using some other Skattish words anaw..

Sha Hoor Sir?   The two Gals thought.. In a Skattish accent..Jist what the fuck is this Beyonce wan up tae ?

But that was Beyoncé's bad news over. .Away doon tae Noo Yoyk..Looking for Tru-Luv. Paid her own coach fair and everything.. Although she had booked an open ended return ticket...The way she had been feeling..

There was only one place she would be going.
.Heaven….Her life had turned pear shaped…. Not even a ride or fuck all… Still.. It was all good news from here on in. .In fact. .It was great news ..But first. .Madge and Rita had some good news of their own to tell.. So Beyoncé asked them what the good news was?

But both the other Gals imagination had been grabbed by the thought of men singing a song?

A song Beyoncé told them they'd heard many a weary homesick Skatsman singing??..Yum Yum..

They demanded to know what the song was she'd heard the men singing?..
But no matter how they tried to spear the arse out her.. Beyoncé wouldn't tell them .Not yet.. She just kept on saying she would tell them later on. .
After they had told her there good news….In fact.. She got so scunnered with them asking.. She eventually snapped at them..

*"Look"* She almost shouted.. *"Stop the fuckin' aboot an' tell me.. Have ye' got good news or no'?.*

*"Oh we've got good news alright"..* Rita smiled.

Madge backed her up.. They had great news...Oh yeah. Great news indeedee...She asked Beyoncé to try and guess where they were going on holiday?

Beyoncé knew the answer to that.. *''Australia''* she told them..

The other pair just stared at her. *.''Australia''* ? Rita asked.

Madonna told Beyoncé they never said they were going to Australia..

Beyoncé insisted they had indeed told her that.  They had indeed...She can well remember the last time she was round they told her ..They were planning to spend all that lovely money they were due from Barry Bang.. Bang ..On taking a month long vacation over Australia. .Gee. They were even practicing their Australian accent and everything..
They were all Kangaroos and Boomerangs at that time.

They were even talking about getting a pushbike each. .A mountain bike..

They were going to start going jogging every day..

They were going to start the Gym and swimming every day....

All in an effort to get themselves in shape for shagging fuck out of Andy Duffy.. All Andy's pals, and all those suntanned surfing dudes on Bonsai beach..

Then after they'd shagged Andy.. His pals and the rest of the male population of Bonsai beach.. They were going to Ayres rock...

Then Madonna remembered.. Aye. .Right enough.. They had indeed said they were going to Australia to shag the utter fuck out Andy Duffy and all his pals.... They had. And Beyoncé was right.. They had indeed been practicing their Australian accents.. But that was before the extra cash they'd got from the scratch card and the miss-sold P.P.I. claim though..

Then Rita remembered as well.. Aye ..They had planned to go to Bonsai beach. Beyoncé was right enough......
.They did tell her they'd be shagging fuck out Andy Duffy.. His pals and all these suntanned surfing dudes.... That would have been great.... But now...Now they had even more lovely cash...They had changed their minds... They were going somewhere truly special. Truly. .Truly special..

*''Aye' We've changed our minds noo though''* Madge told Beyoncé...   *''Nothing wrong with them changing their minds is there.''* ?

'Before Beyoncé had a chance to answer Madge's question.. Rita did..

*''Naw''* she said.. *''Surely It's no' a crime tae change oor minds''*?. .*Cause the world's our oyster,,..*

Was that a statement ? ..Or was that a question?.. It didn't matter, because Beyoncé had to agree..Naw ..She thought. .

The world might be their oyster..

There's nothing wrong with changing their minds. .

It certainly is not a crime to change your mind...In fact. .Beyoncé was changing her mind as well.... Fast...She wouldn't say anything to these pair of selfish Hoors at the moment though. .But she was quickly changing her mind about something….Then she got thinking even further.. Ever since these pair had started growing weed for Barry Bang.. Bang…They had planned to go a lot of places with the cash.. A helluva lot of places. Apart from them planning to go to Australia that is... .

She also remembers the pair of them saying they were heading for Goa. .In the Indian ocean……

Then they changed their minds and were talking about going to Magaluf as well.....Or Shagaluf as Madge had said at the time. ..

They had changed their minds again and were planning to go to Peru. Or maybe it was Nepal?.. Away to the Andie mountains,,. .To learn some sort of mad Yoga thing that Madge had gotten into...And mount all the fit young mountain guys into the bargain.....

Beyoncé even remembers them planning to go to Alaska. .Away shagging all those young Eskimo dudes.. Who hadn't seen a strange woman all their lives..

Another place they talked about going was.. Saudi Arabia.. .Come home dripping in 18 carat gold they said...18 carat gold which was to be donated to them by all these rich young Arab sheiks in return for the Gals sexual favours......

Then they changed their minds once more and were on about taking a round the world cruise. .And they were imagining shagging fuck out all these rich single men who also went on cruises. .Often on their own.

Then they were talking about shagging the male population of the crew on the boat they were planning to take the round the world cruise on. .

Aye.. These pair had changed their minds a lot about where they would be spending all that lovely cash from Barry Bang Bang ...An awful lot.

.But it wasn't a crime to change your mind. .Oh no..

Another thing they were dreaming about was getting a record made. .A song Madonna and Rita had ...Or were thinking about making up together.. They spoke about financing it all themselves. .Putting it You-Tube music and making an absolute fortune. .They were going to be rich and famous pop stars. .Aye. .Right you are..??

Then they were speaking about writing.. Directing and producing their very own movie.. They were going to finance that themselves as well.. With all the lovely cash they were due from Barry..Bang..Bang..

Madge asked Beyoncé what she was thinking about?

Beyoncé told her she was just trying to guess where Rita and her were planning to go on holiday..

*"Oh you'll never.. Ever guess that doll"* Rita told her.. *''Never.''* .She asked Madge to back her up

Madge did.. She told Beyoncé to keep thinking though....

She told her to try and imagine where she would go if she had all that lovely. .Beautiful cash to spend?.

Beyoncé knew exactly where she would go. .In fact…She knew exactly where she was going.. That was all part of her good news.. But she wouldn't be telling these pair anything about it yet .Not yet. .Maybe in a wee while. ? Maybe.? .It all depends….She asked if perhaps they had decided to go away and do some  missionary work.?   .Or Humanitarian work..?

When both the other Gals had stopped laughing Rita told Beyoncé they were both going to be doing their bit for Humanity alright.. ..Once they hit the special place they were going…. They'd be doing their bit for Humanity…Oh yeah…Then …Rita asked her to keep trying to guess where they were off too..

*"It's someplace where we're going to get the arses Rodgered right off us."* Madge added helpfully.. .She asked Rita to back her up..

Rita did. ..Gladly.. She grabbed her crotch and thrust it forward.....*"Oh aye. We're going to get plenty big hard cocks where we're going on holiday'''*..

Then Madge burst into song.. Well not so much of a song, but a few lines of a song they were thinking about making up..

*"Holiday "* She sang.
*''Holiday…We're going away.. Ay'''*

Then Rita grabbed her crotch again and joined in with
   Madge's singing…*''To get the arse shagged off
   us…Every single day.. Ay.''*.

And Beyoncé just smirked to herself....
She hoped they were going to come up with something
   better than that shite for the song they were planning
   to record together ..Aye ..And while they were on the
   subject of recording songs ?..Just wait until these pair
   of selfish Hoors heard her good news. .Because part of
   that involved recording a song... ..It was a real song she
   would be telling them about though.. A real song.. With
   a real recording contract…Not like that shite they had
   just come away with….Maybe she would tell them all
   about it later on .?  .Maybe she wouldn't . .But if she
   did decide to tell them.. They'd be sick as God-Damn
   pigs with no shite to play in....

And that was only a small part of her good news…

Then the joints got passed round. ..As they do all the way
   through the story.  So I won't bore you by keeping
   telling you every time they passed the joints round.
   .Nor will I bore you by explaining every time the Gals
   built another big Grass joint either…But I will tell you..
   The big grass joints got built often.  .They did indeed…

As you will see for yourself if you've been paying attention..

Madge asked if Beyoncé had managed tae guess where they were off too yet.?? ..With them both slipping in the odd Skattish word here and there. .Beyoncé had took a thought about where they were dreaming about going to go this time round.. But she wouldn't suggest it to them. .These pair of dumb cows would never dream about going where Beyoncé was thinking...No way.. Ever. Or maybe aye .. Knowing these pair. .Maybe aye right enough...

So she just answered that she couldn't guess for the life of her...She said Madge would have just to tell her, ..

When Madge told her Leslie Fife. Skatland....Beyoncé acted like she was most surprised...Just exactly what she had been thinking a second or two ago.....It's not as though they hadn't been dropping enough hints or that eh no' ? ..With all these Skattish words an' that ken? ...

*"Sha Hoor..Sir..??* Beyoncé gasped..."*Ye'z are gawn tae Leslie... Fife. .Skatland* "?? ..Leslie..??!!!

Remember she was only acting like she was surprised. .She was onto them ages afore Madge told her.. Aye. .She had been onto them .She'd sort of half guessed they were planning on going to Skatland.. But they weren't onto her.

117

.Were they ?  Naw..The wurrnae…...Just wait until the hear though.. Just wait. .In fact .She had a good mind to tell them right now.. But naw..She'll wait a wee while yet ..Let them blaw a wee while longer….Just wait though…She knew fine the pair were trying to make her jealous. .She knew that fine…But the Beyoncé one wasn't jealous in the least… Normally.. She would have been..

*You would maybe be jealous yourself… If your two best pals were fucking off on Holiday.?  Without you ?…Their best pals who said they were so concerned about  Beyoncé when she was away doon tae Noo Yoyk on her own…....And them with all that lovely spare cash to spend as well…The selfish pair of Hoors..They were thinking they were being smart. .But just wait.....*

But things had changed drastically for the better in Beyoncé's life…Her life had turned full circle….Oh she wasn't jealous….. But she knew fine who the jealous ones would be…Just wait..

Madge begun telling her about how they were both going to do Saint Patricks day in Leslie..

*"The biggest Saint Patricks day parade outside the Island of Ireland"*. Rita added.

They tell Beyoncé all about how they were both going to see Lad-Zones comeback concert at The Quarry Park Belladrome…..They were blawing their load about how they were each paying E.Bay $1000 for a seat in the John Forrest memorial stand.

Then went on about how the both might even be in with a small chance of meeting the boys in the band. .And Beyoncé knew what that meant ..Didn't she??.

They went through what all the thing they would do if they ever got their hands on of any of these guys.

Cowp every fuckin' wan oh them.

Put a shift intae them aw..

When Beyoncé asked if they'd paid for they tickets yet?.. Rita answered they were going to doing just that in the next day or two..

*Just as Beyoncé had thought. The next day or two..??*

Beyoncé asked if they had started the Gym to get themselves in shape for the big holiday..??..

Madge told her they had just decided they'd be better off just waiting until they came home from Skatland before they started the Gym....If they ever came home that is ??

*Just as Beyoncé had thought...She didn't even bothering asking if they had bought pushbikes yet ? .Because she knew fine well what the answer would be..*

Rita told Beyoncé they would be in shape when.   .Or if ,they ever came home from Skatland…She insisted they would be getting shagged so much they would have no time for eating.. Shagging's great for mental and physical exercise she said…

Then they told Beyoncé all about how they were going to see Leslie Hearts playing Barcelona on the Wednesday after the Lad-Zone concert.. They were going to be sitting in the John Forrest memorial stand for that show as well.. Hmmm. .Hmmm

And all Beyoncé said in reply was..'' *Oh that'll be great for you…It''ll be some game. .And you're both huge Leslie Hearts fans as well.. It'll be great…* she told them.. ''Great.''.

Beyoncé knew fine what answer she would get if she asked them if they had booked tickets for this game yet ??

Both the Gals knew Beyoncé loved Leslie Hearts. .Oh Aye….She had the calendar as well.. Oh  My Gawd.. ..Some of the fantasies Beyoncé had about the Leslie Hearts squad were almost biblical in their outrageousness…..And here's them telling her they're both going to see her favourite soccer team…And the Beyoncé one's not even batting an eyelid…They thought she'd be turning green with envy by this time…But no..

Madge looked at Rita. .

Rita looked at Madge..

Both thinking the same thing again...They were both thinking. .This Hoor's taking things very coolly..Too fuckin' coolly .But remember they didn't know Beyoncé's good news.. Did they ?...No they didn't ..But they'd be finding out just shortly though. .In a wee while...

They'd be flying to Skatland with British Airways.. Straight into the Arlene Duffy International airport... .First class....The best of food and as much drink as you wanted.....Nothing but the very best for these two Gals with all that lovely spare cash to spend..

Beyoncé didn't like to ask if they had been onto British Airways to book the first class tickets yet ?...She already knew the answer...That would make it all the sweeter when she told them the rest of her good news.. And they were sitting there trying to make Beyoncé jealous ..Ha.. And just to think.. .She'd only asked the Helicopter pilot to drop her off at Madge and Rita's.... Because she wanted her two pals to be a part of her good news as well...She'd included them in the plans she'd made with her new boyfriend before flying from Noo Yoyk.. Oh she wanted them to be part of her good news alright...She did.. But not now. .Oh no. .She'd finally made her mind up..

Madge suggested they might even Shag somebody on the aeroplane...The pilot maybe.? .Or one of the cabin crew?.

.Or even a stranger they had just new met ?   Join the Mile High Club ?...

And Beyoncé just smirked to herself. They didn't know Beyoncé had already joined the mile high club…. Not long ago in fact. .Of course she had shagged ''*Floyd*'' Her new boyfriends personal chauffeur..

 Her new boyfriend had insisted on an open relationship…He said it was only fair.. With him being away on tour a few month of the year ?? …

And that. .Of course ..Had suited Beyoncé just braw…So of course she'd cowped Floyd, the big black chopper pilot again…

She'd cowped him a good few times before cowping him in the Helicopter.. But that's all part of her good news and you'll hear about that in a wee while.. Anyway.....It had been some task in the Helicopter though.  But she'd managed just fine. .Oh yeah. .She'd managed just fine.....She'd simply sat astride him…. I'm sure you can just picture the sight of Beyoncé thrusting down on Floyds own big black chopper. .And him thrusting upwards.  His free hand all over Beyoncé's tits. ….The other hand trying to keep the other chopper on course… She wouldn't be telling them about anything about that just at the moment though.. That was all part of her good news…And there was more…A lot more….

Just let them keep boasting she thought..

Just let them keep boasting... .

While Madge was still boasting about how great their vacation to Skatland was going to be. .Her and Rita.. Flying ..First class and all the rest of it...Beyoncé reached into one of the bags she had...She brought out a pair of red frilly knickers ..She stood up and slipped the knickers on.. Then she sat back down again.. Without saying a single word...Then she crossed her legs provocatively.. Like Sharon Stone in Basic Instinct.

Aye..   That fairly put a stop to Madge's boasting eh ? ..She stopped in mid rant...

She stared at Rita ..

Rita stared back...Both thinking.. If that Hoor's putting her red frilly knickers back on ?  ...That means she must have taken them off somewhere?.. And they could only imagine where ??.......They wouldn't ask her though.. Oh no....They would both imagine...None of the pair of them would ask though, ..,But that's best pals for you eh ?..How could they nail her to the floor if she told them she'd not long shagged the Helicopter pilot eh ?

The dirty Stop –Oot. ! Madge was thinking..
The cow.! Rita thought.
The slapper !

The Trollop !

The slut !

The lucky.. Lucky fucker...!!!

Beyoncé could feel the envy and jealousy that was reeking
out the pair of these pair.. Reeking out them...She could
feel it in the atmosphere....She knew fine what they
would be thinking..

And they were the ones who trying to make her jealous ?
...

There was silence for a few seconds more while the two
Gals took in what Beyoncé had just done. .Then Madge
continued....She couldn't help herself...She was telling
Beyoncé all about the magical time they were going to
have when they hit Leslie.. All the cocks they were
going to get.. They were even going to have a
competition to see who could shag the most Leslie
boys..   She asked Rita to back her up every time she
mentioned something..  And of course. .Rita did.  Oh
gawd yeah. .They were going to have a great time .

.Rita was also praying Beyoncé wouldn't hang about too
long. .Because Madge had promised to cook that Italian
meal.. Hadn't she..??..And by this time Rita was guttin'
with the Munchies... Guttin' she was..

Beyoncé just smiled at them....

Then the Madonna one. .She asks Beyoncé to imagine if
they met some famous Movie star while they were
visiting Leslie?
*"We'll maybe get a big part in a Movie.. And get our arse
shagged off by all those famous Movie stars into the
bargain"*.. And Rita laughed.....

Beyoncé didn't like to ask if they minded what kind of
Movie they starred in ?....Because she knew the answer
to that as well.. Oh she definitely knew the answer to
that one..

Then Madge Imagined them both meeting a famous Rock
and Roll star ...*"Maybe get us into the music industry eh
Rita ?..Maybe turn us into famous pop stars eh ?"*.

Then Madge jumps up. .She wiggles her arse about a good
bit then starts  singing another wee song.

*"We're saying goodbye to Hollywood"* she sang ...
*'And to the land of Elvis Presley....*
*We're going where life is oh so good...*
.            *We're fuckin' off tae Leslie"*........

No doubt a song she had made up herself.. It had to be..
Because it was shite... Then Rita. She jumps up. She

wiggles her arse about a good bit as well... You saw for yourself the way Madge wiggled her arse about...?..Well.. Rita's copying her...Then she starts singing as well. . Just trying to copy Madge...That was all...Mind you .If Madge told Rita to stick her head in the oven for a while. .Rita would do it. .She would ...If anybody was easily led. .It was Rita....Anyway. .Madge was always encouraging folk to express themselves and that's what Rita was doing... This verse though  ....  It must have been a verse she'd just new made up on the spot...Because it was shite as well...

*"We've had enough of Donald Trump"* Can you hear Rita singing?          .                    *And that auld Hoor ..Bill Clintons wife..*
*They can both go take a pump....*
*Cause we're fuckin' off ..Tae Leslie Fife....*

Then she sang what Beyoncé thought was supposed to be a chorus..

*"Cocks... Whangers ...Willies... Or Dicks ?...* She sang loudly
*"Tadgers... Walllopers.... Bobbies.. Or Pricks...*
*Call them what you wa...ant".*
*"When we hit Leslie... We're going to get them aw...all"*

Then Madge joined in with the chorus as well.. She sang.........                    *"So lock up your sons .When we hit Leslie City... La..La..La..La   La .La...Leslie.!  Leslie.!  .Leslie.!  ..''*

They both let out a right loud Girlie laugh at what they thought was a song.. Then flopped themselves back down on their arses again...They picked up the joints. And started from where they left off. ....Before they had come away with two of the most hideous verses of a song Beyoncé had ever heard....Pure and utter shite. .And these pair of Hoors had visions of being famous pop stars or Movie stars.. ?....Ha ...Beyoncé would give them pop stars and Movie stars alright.. Just wait until they heard the real reason she hadn't been in touch for a whole fortnight...Just wait until they heard how she hadn't sent a text or nothing. .And they'd be gutted when they heard ..As gutted as an old Nun who's Duracel batteries on her favourite vibrator had run flat. .Mid fantasy..Fuckin' gutted..

*''Aye ''* Madge grabbed her crotch ..*''Leslie''* She continued *''Cannae fuckin' wait till we get there .Eh no Ree?..*

Rita of course.. Grabbed her own crotch

*''Too fuckin' right Maddy''* She agreed..''

Then Beyoncé asked if it was just the pair of them that were going to Skatland?...

"Aye" Madge answered ..Just a bit too quickly. ."*Of course we're just going our two selves*".

"*How;*" Rita asked. "W*hat are you asking that for*"?

"*Naw*" Beyoncé answered ."*It's just that*"….Then she hesitated deliberately. Knowing full well the Maddy one would soon fill that silence.. And she did. After only 3 seconds..

"*Just what*" ?  Madonna asked .

"*Just that ah thought you'd maybe take me wi' ye*" Beyoncé answered.. Putting on that sympathetic voice....

 "*You*" Madge spluttered and nearly dropped the joint with the shock of what Beyoncé had just new suggested. .. "*You ? 'You thought we were takin' you tae Skatland wi' us ??*...

"W*hat the fuck wid we want tae take you tae Skatland wi' us fir ?* Rita snapped"...

Beyoncé could answer that in a number of ways...She could tell the reason they hadn't even considered the idea. Oh she knew that fine. .But she just answered it was because she was their best pal….

"*Maybe so*"  Madge said. "*But likesay..It wiz us two who put in aw the hard graft tae get the dosh in the first place. Wizznt it Ree*"..??

Ree agreed.''.*Fuckin' right*'' she said.. *''Aye.. An' we deserve a wee holiday tae oorsel's efter aw that hard work.''*

*You'll have noticed they're all getting right intae their Skattish accents noo...Right intae it.. And you'll know the reason Ree and Maddy are practicing  You know it's because of their big holiday. .But have you taken the time to wonder why Beyoncé is also practising hers ?? Eh ?..Maybe there's something you don't know yet ?..Or maybe you think you've twigged on and are desperate to find out if you've been guessing along the right lines?.. Well you've not long to wait until you find out.*

*One thing you're bound to wondering is.. Just who the hell Beyoncé's new boyfriend is ?..You're bound to be wondering who the hell could aboard his own personal chauffeur to give Beyoncé a lift home in his very own Helicopter ??..Like I says..Haud ye'r Horses and you'll find out in just another wee while..*

Maddy and Ree kept going on about how they deserved a wee stress free vacation to themselves after all the hard work they had put into getting the cash together.. Except for the money from the scratch card and the miss-sold P.P.I claim that is.  .Still. ....Looking after 26 Grass plants for Barry Bang.. Bang was indeed stress-full.. Time consuming work indeed.. They more than deserved their big holiday tae Skatland. .

Both Gals noticed Beyoncé wasn't bothered in the least by this news…Not in the least. .For normal she really would have been distraught…At the very thought of these pair going away without her. .I mean, where was she going to tap some tea bags ?  Or some sugar ?  ..Or some milk? Or a free smoke of weed if these pair were away tae Skatlsand eh ?

Mind you. .That was some bag of weed the Hoor had on her now ??..Where did she get that from ?

Maddy promised they would maybe take Beyoncé with them on their next trip to Leslie. The next time they had a crop of weed ready for Barry Bang.. Bang…They knew fine they would be welcome back to Leslie… Maybe not by the Gals. But the Guys in Leslie would welcome them all back with open arms.

Beyoncé now knew that even supposing these pair had won $50 million on the Euro lottery, they still wouldn't even dream of taking her anywhere with them. No way .Oh she had twigged onto that….And she knew part of the reason as well .Although these pair would never admit it… It was because the guys were all attracted to her dark Latino looks before they would even look at these pair of ordinary white Gals.. Especially that washed up Hoor Maddy…..Maddy ? She Hoor Sir.. She was well named Maddy…And she had the hard neck to say that Beyoncé was away with the fairies, ,Just because she was highly strung. Overly sensitive. .And Beyoncé couldn't help that could she ?..It might have been that she was overly sensitive that she had considered both Madge and Rita in her plans with her new boyfriend ?.Thinking they were her best pals...Ha.. The way these pair were acting.. They were her best of enemies. They'd showed there true colours now alright....... Aye well ..That plan was oot the winndae noo...The selfish pair of Hoors.......Oh It would be Maddy and Ree who would be going round the twist.. Just shortly.   When they found out Beyoncé didn't need them to invite her to Skatland with them...

Madge interrupted Beyoncé's train of thought by telling her that was there good news.. And asking what her own good news was..?

"Aye" Ree said..."Ye' were tellin' us ye' heard men singin'... A song you've heard many a weary homesick Skatsman singin'"

"What song wiz it"?. Madge asked " An who wiz singin"?

And Beyoncé just nodded her head and winked knowingly.. And waited. Leaving that pregnant silence again.. That silence she knew Maddy would be desperate to fill.. And as usual.. She did..

"C'mon tae fuck" She said "Are ye' gawn tae tell us or are ye' no"?

Remember I was telling you earlier on that Madge thought trying to worm anything out the Beyoncé one was sometimes like trying to solve the Times crossword..?. .Well that's just how she was feeling now..

''*Aye*'' Rita added..'' *Tell us what song they men wir singin' B'''*

Knowing they were desperate to find out…B waited another second or two before answering.

''*Caledonia*'' She tells them and smiled widely. *''They were aw singin' Caledonia''*

Madge was just about to ask if it was Skatsmen singin' ? She was just about to ask how many men were there?.. But Rita got in there first..

''*That's wan oh the Skattish songs we've been learnin'..Isn't it Madge''*? She asked.. And that was true .They'd learned a good few Skattish songs off You-Tube since they'd decided they were going on their big adventure to Leslie.. They'd leaned ''*Flower Of Skatland''*..

*''Oh flower of Skatland..*
*When will we see your likes again ''*?

And they'd learned ''*Caledonia*''…Oh Gawd..Yeah.. Of course they'd learned Caledonia….That's the song many a weary homesick Skatsman sung..     They'd often heard stories about how many thousands of these homesick weary Skatsmen sing Caledonia.. With the tears blinding them.. Homesick as anything...But they're still sittin' in their ain Hoose..In Skatland..

*"Oh let me tell you that I love you"*.  These weary homesick Skatsmen sing.. While sittin' in their ain hoose..In Skatland..

*"And I think about you all the time..*
*Caledonia you're calling me ..And now I'm going*
*home.........*

They'd also learned   *"The Road And The Miles To Dundee"*

*"Cauld winter was howlin'..*

*Ower moor and ower mountain"*

And they'd learned *"We're no' Awa' Tae Bide Awa"*..

This was the song the pair planned to sing to all the Leslie Guys when they were leaving their city......They'd even made up another wee verse of their own to add to the end of that particular song.. A wee verse about them going back to about Leslie....O.M.G.  ... They haven't even been there yet and already they're writing songs about them going back..... It goes like this. .See what you think?..

*"Oh we're no awa..Tae bide awa'  ..*
*We're no' awa' tae leave ye'..*
*We're no' awa' tae bide awa'..*
*We'll aye come back an' see ye'..*

*Cause we fell in love with Leslie Town…*
*T'was like being struck by cupid..*
*We always had our knickers down.*
*And the Leslie Guys all shagged us stupid.''.*

It was making up such classic verses like the above that totally convinced the two Gals that one day.. They'd be famous.. On the Telly.. On Top Of The Pops and everything.?? .One day.. Aye. .Even the Spice Girls couldn't write songs as good as that. .Oh ! By the way. .There is an incident involving the Spice Girls in this story. .Well.. One of the Spice Girls anyway.. Posh Spice.. It's about the time her husband, David Beckham, signed briefly for Leslie Hearts .Aye briefly. Because to tell you the honest truth. .His coat had been on a shoogely peg since the very start.. Aye. .It didn't take Craig Noble very long to realise that perhaps he'd made a mistake in signing Becks…

Because..

Just two minutes after signing for Leslie Hearts. Craig had told Becks that he was going to give him the very same gem of advice he gave to all his players. More of a morning Manta, Craig had explained…And that Mantra was. *''First thing in the morning''*, Craig had told Becks. *.''First thing in the morning. . Pull on your socks. .And not on your cocks''*….Becks had been blown away by the pure magnitude of what Craig had just told him. .

Like Craig had just new told him the real meaning of life... Then after a few minutes, Becks answered. *"Yeah Guv"* he'd said in his Cockney accent.... *"Got it Guv. Pull our socks over our cocks ..That's a great piece of advice Guv"* he'd said to Craig.. *'Fookin' great. .Cause it ain't aff' cold up ear innit?...Brass Fookin' Monkey's Guv"*.

And Craig had just shook his head in bewilderment more than anything else....That was the very moment he realised fully why Sir Alex had been so keen to get rid of Becks.

And Craig didn't bother trying to clarify what the team's morning Mantra meant. *"Pull On Your Socks. .And Not On Your Cocks"*

Mind you.. The Becks was the very same in the dressing room. Obviously trying to bond with the Leslie boys. ....When discussing their favourite music and Musicians.. Becks had told the guys he had an epileptic taste in music. (.*He meant ecliptic* )... But was a huge fan of Jazz music more than anything else... .And his favourite Jazz musician was a female singer called *"Elephant."*

The rest of the squad had tried to think. .

And Think

And Think..

But not one of them had ever heard of a Jazz singer called *"Elephant"* before....Not that they were big Jazz fans in the first place like. .They could tell you all about Fat Boy Slim...Puff Daddy. .Rag And Bone Man and all that... .But *"Elephant"* ?  Nut...Naw..

*''Are ye' share* ?'' They'd asked ... But Becks was adamant .....Her name was definitely .*''Elephant''* ..

*''A big Black woman''*.. He'd explained.. Like it was the rest of the squad who were obviously the Dunder-Heeds ...,..

*''Elephant''*!! Becks had insisted.... .*''You moost av eard of er guys. .You moost Av... Elephant Gerald''*!!!.....

 I'm sure I don't have to explain to you Becks really meant... Ella Fitzgerald...

And then. Of course. .We can't forget what Becks had told Craig about his dietary requirements..... He had told Craig that he hated eggs.. Hated eggs with a vengeance. .Hated them.. Couldn't stand the sight of eggs... .He loved omelette though..... Oh yeah. Yum  Yum  .He loved omelette......But he hated eggs..

Becks eh ?.....A wooden headed Hoor of a boy. ...Obviously..

And then of course. .Obviously... There had been two of the most famousist of Beck's comments in his short spell at Leslie Hearts..

It was his first game...Against bitter local rivals, Spartak Kinglassie..An away fixture at Spartak's spiritual home ...The King George V1 stadium..

On hearing he'd been picked for the squad, Becks had told Craig that was joost fookin' great ..Magic... .Couldn't wait to get on the park he said....

And to be playing his first game against the legendary Spartak Kinglassie was an honour indeed. .Mind you..Spartak had tried to sign Becks just a few seasons previously...

Anyway... Craig had told him that if he couldn't cut the mustard.. In other-words.. If he was pish. .He would be getting pulled off at half time..

Becks had been astonished...Truly astonished. ''*Really Guv ?*'' he'd asked in amazement...''*Really*''???

''*Aye really*'' .Craig had replied. .

''*It dizznae matter who the fuck ye' think ye' are*''' Craig had told him....''*Ye'r wi' Leslie Hearts noo ..An' if ye play shite.. We'll pull ye' off at half time*''..

The Becks.. He'd happily told Craig in his cockney accent that was

''*Joost fookin' awesome*''. .*Fookin'.awesome Guv*'' He'd obviously been overcometh with joy. He thought he really had landed on his feet..

Then he'd explained to Craig..

*''Cause wen we was wiff Man United. .We only got aff an owange.''*..

And Craig.?  .Well.. He'd just looked. Then the penny had dropped….And he remembered it was Becks he was talking to…Aye.. Right enough…So he had to put things to him in most simplesteth of terms…And explain he didn't mean .*''You're getting tossed off''* in the way Becks had thought… What he obviously meant was…*''.If you don't play well.. You'll be getting sub'd''* …

 As it turned out. .Becks had to be pulled off long before half time..

 He was indeed shite. .And no match for Spartak's wizards.. The likes of Dod Hunter. Danny Imrie or Matt McGroarty…

Most of the 40 odd thousand visiting Leslie Hearts fans were even Booing Becks..

Willie Latto and John Laing had both ran rings round him.

Kinglassies James Mclay..*( Jacop )*.And Paul Peacock had shown Becks what Scottish football was all about………

That game had ended in a 3-3 draw. …And Spartaks manager..Johnie *( Jap )* Johnston had never been so glad Becks had refused his 35 million pound offer. Never so glad..

Leslie boys still say it was Spartalk's Goalkeeper Freddie ( *The Cat* ) Laing who saved the day for Kinglassie..

Kinglassie boys will argue differently though..

In his interview with the Paparazzi after the game...Becks had told them that it obviously wouldn't have been a draw If either of the teams had scored another Goal or two during the course of the match......

Eh ?. Is that not just brilliant thinking ??

The man must obviously be a pure Genius to have worked that one out.

I think we can safely assume The Becks obviously isn't a honorary Member of M.E.N.S.A''.

But still...On the other hand.. There is one Leslie woman....A Paterson Park woman to be more exact.. She can swear that what some footballers lack in the Brain department. .They more than make up for in the Bobby department..??..Oh aye..

 Posh and Becks had rented a Mansion in Paterson Park you see.. This carry on ended up being named the *''Senga-Gate Affair''*....What a Stooshie that had caused.. When big Senga had kidnapped David.. What a Stooshie.. Polis and awhing.....And if I've got time, I'll tell you much more about that later on.. But for now.. We'll get back to the main story..

Madge had just new asked Beyoncé the question she was going to ask. ."Was it Skatsmen singin' ?.How many men were there"?

Beyoncé told her she would tell her all that in another minute or two ...( *As I was saying...Like trying to solve the Times Crossword.)*..Then she asked the pair if they were certain they weren't going to take her to Skatland with them?..

Once again they told her.. They were certain..100% certain.. They'd already made that crystal clear...

*"Naw...They weren't taking her with them"* Madge snapped...." *Maybe the next time they have a crop ready for Barry Bang  Bang. .They might think about taking her with them then"*..

Madge then told Beyoncé that she's bound to manage to save up some money of her own in the 3 month or so. Until the next crop was ready... They knew Beyoncé growing weed in her own flat was a big No ..No. .Because she was only living in a pokey wee downstairs one bedroom flat.. A private let. .Hardly enough room to swing a cat.. Never mind grow 26 grass plants for Barry Bang..Bang...


*And how Beyoncé was glad this was the case.. She wouldn't want mixed up with the Bang. .Bang clan in any way shape or form. .No way....*

But Madge never knew Beyoncé didn't need to wait until their next crop was ready before she went to Skatland.. She'd find out soon though..

Rita.. She told Beyoncé there was fuck all in Hollywood for them to return home to and they might never come back from Leslie......They might live in Skatland for evermore. ? Meet some rich Dude and Emigrate.?.. And if that were to be the case.. Then they would send Beyoncé some *"I love Leslie"* T-Shirts over.. They would send her The *"I love Leslie"* Baseball caps as well.. She'd also be more than welcome to fly over and visit them in Leslie anytime she wanted...More than welcome.. ..She asked Madge to back her up.. But Madge never said a word. Not a cheep did she say.. Because she was to busy thinking. .Thinking that this Hoor Beyoncé has something up her sleeve....So Rita continued telling Beyoncé once again that they weren't taking her with them this time.. Oh no.. This was a big treat for them both..

Then Madge butted in.  Once again she asked if the men she heard singing were Skatsmen?..How many men were there?

*"I'll tell ye'z in a minute "* Beyoncé answered. *" After ah asked ye' wan mair time..Yooz are sure ye'r no' taking the Beyoncé one tae Skatland wi' ye'z eh no'?. .That's ye'r minds made up eh ?*

141

Madge just groaned heavily in annoyance.. How many times had they told her now eh?. .She was just going to ask that, but before she had a chance to speak, Beyoncé continued..' *Naw...Are ye'z fuck..Ye'z never even had me in ye'r plans fir gawn tae Skatland wi' ye'z.... Did ye ?? Same as ye'z never had me in ye'r plans when ye'z were gawn tae Australia or nuhing did ye'' ? ..''Naw .''Did ye'z fuck..*

*"Aw fuckin' listen tae her"* Madge said to Rita and nodded in Beyoncé's direction.... *"Listen tae her. .Poor Beyoncé eh ?.Poor Beyoncé...Well you can go an' fuck.. Cause we're no' takin' ye' ..   Right !!!? Get that intae ye'r thick fuckin' heed.. Save up ye'r ain money an' ye' can maybe come wi' us the next time..*

Before Madge got any further with her outburst, Rita interrupted. Telling Beyoncé once again that if they decided to locate to Leslie..?. Then she was welcome to visit any time she fancied she asked Madge to back her up.. But Madge never said a word in reply....

Beyoncé asked if they'd managed to get a passport yet?.. Although she knew the answer full well. .And she was right, because Rita answered with a ..*"Naw"* .Then Madge told Beyoncé they would get their passports at the same time as they booked the British Airways tickets..

Beyoncé asked if they had booked any accommodation in Leslie yet?

They pair told her the choice of Hotels in Leslie were overwhelming and they hadn't made up their minds where they were going to stay yet ..But they would get all that fixed out very soon.. It would be somewhere posh as fuck though.. Oh yeah ..With all that ready cash to spend.. They wouldn't be choosing anywhere down market. .That was for sure. .But they'd get all that fixed out ..At the same time as they were organising their passports..

Beyoncé told them calmly that it could take over 6 weeks to receive a passport.. That's if you had ever filled in the passport application form in the first place...She asked if any of the pair of them had filled in their passport application forms yet ?..She asked if any of the pair of them had even got as far as having their photos taken for their passport application forms yet ?

And of course.. The answer was just as Beyoncé had expected...They would get all that fixed out just shortly.. *"Maybe Rammoara eh Ree"*? Madge asked Rita and Rita took another huge sook out her Grass joint before answering...*"Yeah"* she agreed. *"Yeah indeed.. .. Maybe Rammoara"*....

*Gee. .The nearer the time came for these two Gals big adventure to Leslie.. The better their Skattish accents were becoming.. What dae hink yersel' noo? ....Sha Hoor Sir....It sounds a lot better than when they first started anyway. .Likesay..There's hardly any notice of Madge's American*

143

*accent noo.. And even better. .Hardly any trace of Rita imitating Madge's American accent. .In that fake false annoying way that a lot of people seem hell bent on imitating nowadays..*

Although she knew the answer full well.. Beyoncé asked if any of the pair had done anything about getting driving lessons fixed out?  Had they applied for their provisional driving licence yet ?

Madge had her answer ready though.. She pointed out that there was no point in doing all that until the decided if they were coming home from Skatland or not...You couldn't drive on Skattish roads with an American licence. They drove on the other side of the road.....If they did stay in Skatland as planned ?..Then they would get all that fixed put then. Get themselves a Skattish driving licence.. Then get themselves a shaggin' wagon each. Madge asked Rita to back her up.. And of course, she did.. Oh yeah ..

Then Madge told Beyoncé to never mind about their lives ..She was getting off the subject of the men singing *"Caledonia"*. .What aboot that she asks?

Beyoncé.. She tells Madge that she's only got wan mair question tae ask them then she'll tell them aw aboot the men singin'..

Madge sighs in exasperation...And tells Beyoncé she hopes to fuck she's not going to ask if they're taking her to Skatland with them?...Cause the answer's still Naw !!!

Beyoncé tells them she wasn't going to ask them about that again. .Oh no.. It was crystal clear they had no intention of even considering that..

She was actually going to ask when was the last time any of the pair of them had their Hole?  Then she answered her own question by telling them it was the last time the councils Gas engineer had been round to service the boiler..

*"Wiz it fuck"* Madge screamed.

*"No it wizznae"* Rita screamed even louder…*"We've both had oor Hole after that haven't we Madge"*?

Madge of course agrees. *"Aye Hiv we".. We've both had oor Hole efter we cowped Rab Hood awright"*

Then Beyoncé laughs and tells them if that wasn't the last time they'd had their Hole?.. Then it would be when Quinny..The window cleaner had been round..

*"So what "*?.Madge snaps *"So fuckin' what"* ?..

And Rita.. She has another huge sook on her big Grass joint. .But she never said a word. .But she was thinking. .When Madge and Beyoncé are at each and other's throats like this. .It's like a human version of duelling Banjos..Tellin' ye' man….

*Madge had surely forgot all about. .Kevin White.. The Council Joiner…So I'll wait and tell you about that later on..*

145

And because Madge had forgot all about Kevin..

The Council Joiner.. Beyoncé thought her guess had been right enough..…..

*'''You went away doon tae Noo Yoyk didn't ye'''* Madge rants on…'' *An' you never got ye'r Hole either did ye'?…..''So dinnae you sit there an' ask us aboot the last..''…..*

Beyoncé cuts her off.. Mid conversation…''*Who says ah never got ma Hole like''*? She asks and sort of half laughs at her own question. .

If only they knew.? .

If only?

The pair of sex starved, frustrated, selfish Hoors, were about to find out now though..…..

*''Ah only says ah never cowped Robbie.. The Artist''* She tells them*..''* .*But ah never said ah didnae get ma Hole did ah''? ..Oh Sha Hoor sir. .Ah got ma Hole awright..''* She smiles at the Memory…

*''Aw aye''* Madge shouts trying not to sound jealous ….
*''Aw aye.. Next you''ll be tellin' us ye' kissed a Frog that turned intae a rich young Hunk oh a Prince who wiz hung like a Donkey.''*

*''Ah'd have been as well''* Beyoncé replied..
*''Hmmm..Hmmm''*

146

Madge continued.. Still trying to spear the arse out Beyoncé... *"Or have ye' met some Dude who's won the Euro Millions or something eh "*?

*''Like ah says''* Beyoncé smiled....*''Ah'd  have been as well''*...

*"Has this got tae dae wi' the men who were singin''Caledonia like?''* Madge asked.. ……How many times has she asked that now ?..You'd think she was desperate to find out eh ?.

*''It was indeed''* Beyoncé  purred in reply *''It was indeed''*

*"Moan Nen ..Spill the fuckin' beans ''*   Madge nearly jumped down Beyoncé's throat... .*''Who have ye' been cowpin' ?*....

*''Ah'll tell ye' the full story first''*  Beyoncé replied...*''Mind ah wiz telling' yen's ah wiz sitting' on the rocks at the sea shore eh''* ?  *That wiz when ah heard the men singin''''*....

*"Aye.  ''*..Rita answered.. She was getting as desperate as Madge to hear the full story..

''*Well*'' Beyoncé continued... They saw suddenly stopped singing' When wan oh them asked if they all fancied a bit oh skinny dipping'?

''*Away an' fuck*'' Madge said. ''*Year dreaming' ya' daft Hoor*''

*Oh um ah? Um ah? Well wait till ye' hear this fir dreamin'''*....Beyoncé continued.. *"They aw stripped aff.. The lot.! .Socks.! .Shoes !.Shirts ! !.An' Kilts..!!*

*"They were aw wearin' kilts"* ? Rita gasped. Nearly slavering at the mouth..

''*Yep*'' Beyoncé answered..''*An they aw ran intae the water..Splashin' aboot.... But it must have been frozen cause they were aw shoutin' aboot the water freezin' the baws aff ye'.. So they aw turns roond tae run back oot...Bollock naked...An' there wiz me sittin' there aboot ten feet away..*''.

And Rita just sat open mouthed..
Madge never said a word either. .But you'll know all the questions they were dying to ask eh?
But Beyoncé carries on with her story.. She tells them Dougray shouted that there was a Mermaid sittin' on the rocks.

*"Dougray who"*?   Madge asked...There weren't many folk called *"Dougray"* going around....In fact.. Madge had only heard of one person by that name.. He was a big proud Hunk of a Skattish Actor who was in Mission Impossible..Sodjer..Sodjer... And all that.....She was praying The Beyoncé one hadn't met the Dougray she was thinking of.?   Surely no'.........But she had, Or so she said.. Because Beyoncé answers..*"Dougray Scott.. Who the fuck dae ye' think".? '.*

And Madge shivered like somebody had just new walked over her Grave.....Oh.. The fantasies she'd had involving Dougray Scott.. Oh Sha Hoor Sir ..What. ?   .In fact.. Her knickers were getting moist at the very mention of his name...It was rumoured that Dougray's mum used to lift him out his cot and his pram by the Cock...Seemingly...That's the excuse he gave the Gals to explain its size... When Madge was younger. Her sexual fantasies always involved rodgering another Skatsman.. Big Sean.. Sean Connery.. But as Big Sean had got older ..And so had Madge.. Although Big Sean still made an appearance now and again.. It was Big Dougray Scott who had taken over from Sean. .Oh how Madge loved to give her fanny the thousand rubs fantasising about Dougray's Big hard Skattish cock hammering between her legs....  But the thought of Dougray and Mel

Gibson.. At the one time.. Spit roasting her and awhing..And Mel's wearing his kilt and has his face all painted like he did in Braveheart..And they could sing *"Caledonia"* all they fuckin' wanted.. Shout *"Freedom"* or anything..

But without waiting on any kind of smart reply, Beyoncé tells them Dougray had shouted to Mel that there was a Merm...

*"Mel"* ? Rita interrupts.. *"Ye' mean Mel?...Mel"* ??
*'Aye"* Beyoncé answers *"Mel.. Mel Gibson"*..

Rita was just about to ask how many men were there altogether ?  ..
She was just about to ask if there had been any more Skatsmen..?..But Madge jumps up. .Can you see her?.. Waving her arms about in frustration and shouting at Rita not to listen to Beyoncé..
She's shouting at Beyoncé that she's nothin' but a Haiverin' Hoor. .A Blether. .
She told Beyoncé she was nothing; but a Dreamer...She's shouting that Beyoncé never met Dougray Scott and Mel Gibson. .She was a Fantasist.. Walter fuckin' Mitty... Smoking too much weed Madge told her....Livin' in Alice In Wonderland...  Then Madge flops herself back down on her chair..

But the huge smile on Beyoncé's face told Rita that perhaps she was telling the truth ?  ....Rita wasn't so convinced Beyoncé was a Haiverin 'Hoor after all....And it's not just that. .If she was telling the truth ?.Then she was one lucky fucker of a Gal. .Oh aye. .Now she was talking.. Because Rita would do anything to meet Dougray Scott. ..The Big Skattish Hunk....Anything...Dougray often featured in Rita's sexual fantasies when she was dreaming about all the Movie stars she would ride. .And although Mel Gibson was getting a wee bit over the hill now. .She'd still put a shift intae him...But her favourite sexual fantasies involved Big Dougray Scott and another Movie star,...It was another Hunk of a Skatsman..Another James Bond in fact. ...Daniel....Daniel Craig.. Oh Sha Hoor Sir.. The things she would do to Daniel and Dougray if she ever got her dirty paws on them. ..And here's Beyoncé telling them Big Dougray's standing right in front of her. Bollock naked?  Wearing not a stitch ?   And he's shouting to Mel Gibson in that Sexy Skattish accent that there was a Mermaid sittin' on the rocks.. If only it had been Daniel Craig instead of Mel...Ohhhhh  !!  .Rita had to stop her left hand from sub consciously moving to between her legs...She's also wishing she really was Beyoncé's bestest pal in the whole wide world.

.If Beyoncé was telling the truth that is ??..And although she would never admit it.. Madge would be wishing the very same thing..

Rita must have been so caught up in own thoughts that she never heard what Beyoncé said next.. Because the next thing she knew. .Madge had lowped up out her chair again.. And she's going psycho at Beyoncé ..Shouting that she's worse than Walter Fuckin' Mitty for blethering pish. .She's shouting that Beyoncé's just coming away with all that crap because she's trying to make her and Rita jealous .Just because they're going on Hoilday to Skatland and they're not taking her with them.. *''Dougray Scott''* ? She's asking.. *''Mel Gibson'*? *And noo you're expecting us tae believe that Daniel Craig's wiz skinny dippin' anaw? Standin' right there in front oh ye' ..  Bare naked. ? Pish''* Madge is shouting .*''.Fuck right off....Ye'r livin' in the land of make believe..Bletherin' a load oh shite..*

*'' Ah'm ah fuck bletherin' shite''* Beyoncé insisted. *.''Not at all''* she says...*''Wait till ye' see this.''*.. She tells Madge.. Then she reaches into her M.K Handbag. .

Rita's ears have fairly pricked up now though ?..I'm sure you know what she was fantasising about now eh ?..Oh Sha Hoor Sir.. Aye... .All these big Skattish whangers just hanging there. .Right in front of you? ..Fair enough.. Mel's not really a Skatsman..But his Granny was Skattish…. And as Mel had proved in Braveheart..He can make a not bad job of a Skattish accent...So that would qualify for being a Skatsman in Rita's books..... Anyway. .The thought of Big Dougrays..Daniel Craigs and Mel Gibsons tadgers......... Probably within arms reach  ???.....And didn't Rita love a Skatsman. ??..She would be at a loss what one to reach out for first. …But then again. .She's got two welcoming hands.  .Hasn't she ??...And once more. .She had to stop one of them slipping subconsciously between her legs..

Madge flops herself back down again…She's silent for a wee second or two..   But Beyoncé knew fine Madge was trying to act like she was bylin' mad. .Just to cover up for the jealousy that was pouring out her….She couldn't exactly admit to feeling jealous , could she ?..Naw..Could she hell.. Especially after her futile attempts to make Beyoncé jealous just a wee while ago…. But Beyoncé would rub it right in.. Oh aye.. Madge would even more jealous in just a second or two…..

Beyoncé brings her phone out of her M.K. Handbag ..She swipes the screen a few times then asks the pair to look at that....She passes the phone over.. Rita reaches out and takes a hold of it.... She gazed at the screen. .And her tongue nearly hit the floor.

Can you hear the Gasp she's just new let out ?.. O.M.G.. she gasps.. O. .M. Fuckin'. .G !!

Because the first thing that went through her mind was..Sha..Hoor .Sir. .It's true enough about Dougrays mum lifting him out the pram by his Bobby. What a size of a whanger...Like one of those Cumberland sausages hanging there.......And right enough.. Standing next to Dougray was Daniel Craig and Mel Gibson ..And not only that.. There was another 3 men in the picture as well....Rita recognised every one of them immediately.. Every single one....

One was Jason Momoa..Who they'd seen in ''*Game Of Thrones*''. .

Another was Jamie Dornan. Who starred in'' *50 Shades Of Grey*''. ..

The Dude standing on Mel's left hand side was Gerard Butler.....

Every single Movie star Rita had ever fantasised about riding..

And they're all bare naked…And they're all big boys in the cock department….Beyoncé said they had all stripped off their kilts to go skinny dipping, just a wee while ago.. They were all still soaking wet…The same way as Rita's knickers were starting to feel.. The sight was almost too much for her.. She licked her lips ..Imagining herself being sandwiched in between all these Big Hunky stars of the Movie world.. And most of them Skatsmen into the bargain…….She could feel beads of sweat beginning to form on her forehead….. She must have stared at the screen for much longer than she thought. Because the next thing she knew.. Madge had taken the phone from her.. She looks at the screen for a second or two…. Taking in that most beautiful of sights.. Then she shouts at Beyoncé that she must think the pair of them are fuckin' daft. .

Madge said Beyoncé had downloaded the photo from the Internet. Either that or somebody had photo-Shopped it and posted the image to her..

*"Ye must think we've got "Mug" written aw ower oor heeds"* Madge told Beyoncé.

Beyoncé reached out for her phone and told Madge nobody had sent the image to her ..She said it was herself who took the photo. .She started swiping the screen again..

Madge sill insisted Beyoncé was a blethering Hoor and asked what the fuck all those Movie stars would be doing gathering in Noo Yoyk in the first place.??

Beyoncé answered that they were all there to celebrate the birth of Rod Stewart's new born bairn.. They were ower *''Tae Wet The Bairns Heed''* as Dougray had explained in that Sexy Skattish accent..

Beyoncé said all the Guys were full of sympathy when she'd told them the reason why she was sitting on these rocks greetin' her Een oot in the first place..

Rita asked hopeingfully if they were all still Bare Naked?

*''For a wee while''* Beyoncé answer back.

She said when the Dudes were getting dressed again. Gerard had said.... ''
*''Ye' must be frozen sittin' there Darlin'''* ..Then he'd given her his shirt to put on..
And Dougray..He had wrapped his coat around her shoulders....
*''Jist tae keep ye' warm Doll''* He had told her....
.Beyoncé explained they had all invited her back to a party at Calvin's pad..

*''Calvin who''* Madge enquired then answered her own question by saying ;*''Calvin Klien''* ?..Then she laughed that false condescending cackle.. Exactly the same way a lot of folk at the Amateur Dramatic Clubs laugh..

Rita wasn't laughing though. .Oh no. .Wiz she fuck laughing. .She was experiencing the horrifying flashbacks. Terrible.. Dreadful memories were coming back to disturb her...She squeezed her legs and arse cheeks tightly at the very mention of Calvin Klien..Because. .Remember a wee while ago, I explained to you about just how much Justin Timberlake had pleaded with Rita to shave her Toosh for him ?..Do you remember that ?..And after Rita had finished with the Gillette and everything was braw and smooth. .Do you remember she had splashed a big handful of Justin's aftershave on her bare Toosh.. Well it had been Calvin Klien aftershave that she'd splashed on. .Remember she'd felt like somebody had been at her Fanny with a blowtorch ?..She'd thought her Fanny was on fire ? And she'd splashed the cold water on ... The beads of sweat really were running down her forehead at the memory.. Oh Sha Hoor Sir. .Never again !! .Never ever again !!!..Never !!!!

Well Maybe ?

Maybe ??

Maybe if the likes of Big Dougray or Gerard Butler or Jason or Mel asked her nicely.??... She would consider shaving her Toosh for them. .Her imagination was running wild at the very thought.. Gawd...She would crawl over a mile of broken bottles just to see the sparkle off these guys pish......So aye.. Maybe ?.... She definitely wouldn't be using the aftershave this time round though.  .Rita relaxed a wee bit.. She was still sweating though. .Maybe...By this time. it wasn't the memories that were making her sweat so much she thought to herself..??

It wasn't Calvin Klien Beyoncé was on about anyway.. It was Calvin Harris..

''*Pish*''Madge shouted.. ''*Push*'   She was certain Beyoncé was just using Calvin Harris's name because she knew fine well Madge would love to cowp him...Oh Sha Hoor Sir.. Aye. ..When she was having her extremely vivid and unbelievable sexual fantasies about all the Big Skattish Rock stars she would love to ride......Calvin was nearly top of her list ....Nearly.. Rab Broon.. George Thompson and the rest of the guys from Lad-Zone were at the very. .Very top. But even still, when giving her pussy the thousand rubs . .Dreaming about her putting a shift intae all the Lad- Zone Dudes...Calvin often made a cameo appearance…Oh Aye. .Often…And she knew Rita felt the same way….. But she shouts at Beyoncé..''Pish..

''Naw..No' pish'' Beyoncé smiles…'Look" She says and hands her phone back over..

Madge takes a look at the screen.. Then she draws daggers at Beyoncé…It was more like Claymores she was drawing.. Aye Claymores….
Rita thought that if looks really could kill?. .Then Beyoncé would be dead a Hundred times over..

Beyoncé…She smirks over at Rita. .She nods her head shrewdly and she winks as if to say.. ''Watch this ''.

There was utter silence in the room ..Utter silence…..Writers would describe it as a pregnant silence….Rita knew it must have been something appetising Madge was looking at on the screen though. .Because she noticed her tongue flick in and out a few times involuntary.. ..That's right.. Just the way you're imagining….You're maybe even practicing it ??….. Like a month old kitten licking a saucer full of milk.. That's it. You've got it spot on..

.''What dae ye' hink oh that photie then Madge Doll'' ? Beyoncé asked after nearly 15 seconds…..15 seconds might not seem a long time.. But if you count it out in your head..15 seconds is a helluva long time for a silence to be pregnant .Especially with the atmosphere being as tense as it was. .And you already know. .Madge doesn't like long silences……But anyway. Beyoncé tells Madge…. *"That proves ah'm no' bletherin' pish ataw eh"?*

Madge hands the phone over to Rita..
She stares at the screen ..Then over at Beyoncé.. Who just winked and smiles again…. Rita stares at the screen once more…It was just as well she was sitting down. Otherwise her legs would have completely folded beneath her.. Because there was the bold Beyoncé on the screen. Sandwiched between Dougray.. Gerard and Jason.. Not sitting on a couch or anything like that.. Oh no .This photo had been taken in a bedroom….They're all bare naked…..Beyoncé was bent over double..Dougray was behind her.. ..It was perfectly obvious he had that big Cumberland sausage rammed in between her legs…
She had Jason Mamoa's cock in one hand ..In the other hand she held Gerard Butlers whanger.. Although it was clearly evident by the torrent of spunk pouring out of her mouth and the huge smile on the lucky Hoors face what had been going on..

Rita.. She had to sit on her free hand.. Otherwise it would have been wandering involuntary.  And you know fine well where it would be wandering to.. Don't you ?..... She looks at Madge.. Who is already staring at her...That Telepathy I was telling you about earlier on was at work again...And I'm sure you don't need me to explain all these thoughts that were being transmitted on the Telepathic airwaves..

Beyoncé reaches out and asks Rita to pass her phone back.
Rita does.. That left both hands free, and you're right....She had to stop them wandering. .Because you've got to admit. ..That was some sight she'd just new seen..Sha. .Hoor ..Sir. It wasn't half..

Beyoncé.. She taps and swipes the screen again... Telling the pair if they think that photie was good.? .Then wait until they see the next one....Then passes the phone back over to Madge....And sure enough.. The very Skatsman who often made a cameo appearance when Madge was having those extremely vivid sexual fantasies about all the Skattish Rock stars she would cowp was standing right there.. Calvin Harris. ...He's replaced Dougray....And he's also got his big hard Skattish cock rammed between Beyoncé's legs... While Mel Gibson and Daniel Craig had replace Jason and Gerard.. They're bare naked as well..

And the very same as in the previous photo. .Beyoncé was covered in spunk..Laggered with it she was.... It was dripping out her mouth. .Running down her chin ..It was all over her hair...And of course... That jammy Hoor. .Beyoncé... Had a smile on her face like the cat who really had got the cream...Mind you.. All the guys were smiling as well..

Madge licked her lips and Rita had just new leaned over and looked at the screen.. When Beyoncé. .She gets up. .She takes her phone from Madge.. *"Watch this"* She tells them. .*"Watch this"*.. She taps and swipes the screen again.. Then after a second or two they could hear the sound of grunting and moaning...And screams of pleasure . Beyoncé hands her phone to Rita then goes and sits back down.. Madge leans over to get a better look...It's a video.. A video starring Beyoncé.. She's thrusting herself down on Jamie Dornan's cock. She's facing forward.. Jamie's big hands are rubbing spunk into Beyoncé's tits.

She's got Dougray's big Cumberland sausage in one hand..

She's got Calvin Harris's cock in the other hand.. Wanking them both furiously...

And in her mouth she's got somebody else's cock..??..

162

Somebody else the two Gals hadn't seen before.. Madge couldn't help herself but ask who it was.

*''Who's the big black Dude''*? She asks Beyoncé..

He was indeed a big black Dude...A big black muscle bound Hunk. .His dreadlocks swinging wildly as he thrust that big hard black whanger in and out of Beyoncé's mouth..
Can you hear Beyoncé screaming and moaning with ecstasy and gratification?

*''Aw.. That's Floyd''* Beyoncé tells them. *''.Floyd's Calvin's personal chauffeur.. Just when Calvin's in America like..* And she smiles....*''Floyd's a big boy, Eh''*?

Floyd was indeed a big boy Rita thought in a Skattish accent..Oh..Sha..Hoor..Sir..... Aye. Floyd's big boy awright..

Talk aboot a big raw black pudding.? .

Talk aboot Ebony and Ivory?

The Ivory being Jamie Dornan..

Then of course.. The Ebony.. Big black Floyd in front of her..

And Ebony and Ivory were working in perfect harmony ? Perfect.. Jist braw and Dandy..

The Gals were still taking in the vision when Dougray shoots his load all over Beyoncé...He let out an ear piercing screech of pleasure.. Can you hear him ?. ''Ahhhhhh.''.. He went. ''Ohhhhhh... Ohhhhhh''.( .*Sounding very much like the Lord Mayor of Leslie when Cinders is licking the Strawberry flavoured yoghurt off his sausage.*).

This was followed closely by Calvin coming.. He screams with satisfaction as his spunk shoots all over Beyoncé....

 And Jamie.. He's still rubbing the spunk into Beyoncé's tits..
She couldn't even lick the come from her chin.. Because wasn't her mouth full of Floyd's big black cock.??..Then Floyd had also let out a squeal of enjoyment. And you know what happens next ..Don't you ?  .Talk about a flood ?   Gawd... Beyoncé had nearly chocked on it.. Pouring out of her mouth like fuckin' Niagara Falls it had been......

Then Daniel Craig swaps places with Dougray.. Dougray's panting like he's just finished running a Marathon..

Jason. .He takes Calvin's place....Jason's sweating like he's been running away from the Police..

Gerard Butler. He replaces Big Black Floyd.. The Helicopter pilot. .And Floyd's smiling like he's just had the best B.J. he's ever had in his whole life..

They could see Mel standing in the background....Just waiting to take his turn..

Beyoncé... She's still thrusting up and down on Jamie Dornan's cock..
And they're all away again.. More or less recreating the previous scene..

And if you thought the atmosphere earlier on was tense then you should feel it now..Gawd you could slice it with one of those Claymores I was on about a wee while ago.. The vibes pouring out of Madge were.. Jealousy.. Oh aye.. Definitely jealousy and Envy.. Would you not be jealous and envious if your so called best pal was shagging all those stars of the Movie and Music world?..

Resentment?.. Definitely Resentment...But would you not resent your so called best pal shagging all those stars

..Who you'd often fantasised about shagging yourself
?..Often. .Last night in fact..

Hatred maybe ?...Well Aye.. But would you not hate your
best pal.  If she was getting all that cock... And you
weren't ?

One thing was certain. The Madonna one was as sick as a
pig..
As sick as a dog in a street with no lampposts...
With Beyoncé being a sensitive kind of Gal. .She could pick
up on all those bad vibes.. No problem….And these pair of
slappers thought they were Telepathic ?..Ha… .And the
Telepathic vibes ripping out of Madge were indeed bad..

Beyoncé knew fine well that inside Madge's heart and
inside her head she would be going Psychopathic.. Not
Telepathic ..Aye well. Fuck her.
She deserves it.. Trying to crucify Beyoncé with smart
comments.

*"Ye'd think "Robbie".. The Artist, would take their new
found love fir a slap up meal tae K.F.C. instead oh
MacDonald's .Eh "? She'd sniggered hadn't she ?*

Hadn't her and Rita buckled up when she told them about
Robbie pishing himself ?  Aye had they. .

And hadn't they laughed when she told them about him being sick all over the top of her. ? .Aye..

They'd laughed even louder when she'd told them about Robbie shitting himself..

*"Is it Calvin Klien's party ye've been invited back tae"?* Madge had cackled in that way I was telling you about.. Like the folk at the Amateur Dramatic Clubs..

Aye   Fuck them. .They deserve to have their noses rubbed right in it.. And there was more to come.

Beyoncé could tell that Madge would love nothing more than to take Beyoncé's phone and throw it against the wall.. Jump on it. .Stamp fuck out the phone until it was on the Blink altogether...She would love to jump up and skart Beyoncé's Een oot... Madge maybe wouldn't say so. .Oh no. But Beyoncé could tell.. Like I says.. She's a sensitive Gal..

She also knew the pair wished they hadn't been so fuckin' smart when Beyoncé had asked if she was included in their plans to go to Skatland.?..But she wouldn't be asking them again. .Like I was telling you...There's more to come.. And in just a wee while ....When Beyoncé tells them ..It would be these pair of jealous Hoors who would be begging Beyoncé to take them to Skatland with her. .She'll tell them all about that very shortly though..

*''They're ye' go Madge''* Beyoncé says.. *''That proves ah did get ma Hole in Noo Yoyk ''...*

And Madge. .She just glowers.. Can you see her face.? .It's like a Bulldog chewing a Mouth-full of wasps..

Then Beyoncé reaches out and asks Rita to pass her phone back over..
Rita does and while Beyoncé's is tapping and swiping the screen, she tells them that particular Fuck –Fest had only lasted 3 days then the rest of the guys had to go home for one reason or another..
She explains that had just left her and Calvin.. Just the pair of them..
She tells them Calvin had revealed that he'd fell in love with her with her the second he'd clapped his Een on her…
He'd been drawn to her like a magnet.
Like a moth unto a Flame he'd said..
Their meeting had been written in the stars he'd told her…
Fate..
They were each other's destiny.....

.Love at first sight he'd promised ..
He was crazy in love now..
And he'd told her all this even after she'd shagged him..
So that just goes to prove he was telling the truth ..
Cupid had fired his arrow Calvin had told her.. A few
minutes after Calvin himself had fired his load..

Cupid had fired his arrow and it had struck them both in
the heart..

And hadn't Beyoncé felt exactly the same way ??....

Hadn't she came all the way to Noo Yoyk on the
Greyhound coach looking for Tru-Luv ??..Paid her own fair
and everything ..And look how things had turned
out.....Yep.. Their meeting had most definitely been
written in the stars. .Fate indeed. .Destiny..

Madge asked if Calvin didn't mind her shagging all these
other Guys?

*"Not at all* ".Beyoncé answers. *"Not at all"*.
Then she tells them just what I told you just a wee while
ago. Calvin was a huge Advocate of Girl Power, and he
had insisted on an open relationship, because he didn't
think it was right and proper for Beyoncé to go without
her Hole. While he's away on tour for 2 or maybe 3

months of the year.. But aye. Calvin. .Beyoncé's new found B.B.F. was all for Girl Power..

Now.. At this point. .Beyoncé fully expected Madge to suggest that Beyoncé should tell all these Guys she was pregnant...Pregnant.. And didn't know who the Father was...Suggest to them they should each send her a huge big whack of cash each. ..*A HUGE BIG WHACK*...Otherwise.. She would go to the Paparazzi with the photos and the Video...Say the Guys had all taken advantage of her.. That she was an unwilling participant in all this...Oh aye.... That's the sort of scam Madge would entice Beyoncé into...In fact.. Madge would cajole anybody into any sort of scam going.. The scamming Hoor..That's what she was.....But no.. The bold Madge never uttered a word in that direction..

It will have become very evident throughout this story that.. Just like Calvin.. Both Madge and Rita are also huge advocates of ''GIRL POWER''...Of course they were...Gawd Yeah.. They had realised years ago the time when woman were tied to the kitchen sink were well gone..  Also gone were the days of Guys thinking they could use Gals as nothing more than sexual playthings...Ha...It was the other way around nowadays...Gals ruled the world.. *''Gal Powah''*..Oh Gawd Yeah .It was Gals who now wore the trousers now my lad.... Not half.. And so what if Guys called Gals a shower of sexist pigs.. So what?.  Gals certainly didn't….The tide had turned rapidly in that direction. .And Gals round the whole wide world were realising it..  Some sensible guys.. Like Calvin , were beginning to understand that you couldn't hold back the tide..  ..Could you.?. No you couldn't……And you couldn't turn the tide back either…

**''.GIRL POWER''.!!!!!!!.**

*"Sisters were doing it for themselves..*
*Standing on their own two feet and ringing their own bell''..*

Big Dougray.. Gererd Butler.. Big Black Floyd and the rest of these Dudes may think they were using Beyoncé…But you've just new seen the video for yourself, and I'm sure you agree, It was the other way round. Totally the opposite. ..You saw for yourself who was having the most fun didn't you ?.. **''GIRL POWER''**…As the Spice Girls used to sing.. Aye .But.. .Here…It was another story altogether with Posh …Sha ..Hoor ..Sir. .It wizznae half…
When the trusty officers from the L..P.D ( *Leslie Police Department* ) Discovered her Hubby,  David, handcuffed to Big Senga's bed.. With one of Big Senga's black fishnet stockings rammed in his mouth ..To prevent him from screaming.....Aye......For 3 whole days and 3 whole

nights…. Big Senga had shown David what Girl Power was all about.  ….*Paterson Park Stylee…*

Aye. .The Posh had changed her mind about Girl Power then alright…. What a state she got herself intae…

And that's how the *"Senga –Gate Affair"* had first come to the public's attention. .But like I keep saying.  I'll tell you more about *"The Senga Gate Affair"* later on .

 And I'll tell you more about Big Senga's reply when Posh had called her a Hoor…Oh you'll laugh at that…One thing I can tell you at the minute. .Is ..Big Senga had told Posh that she'd taken 3 nights off from The Bingo..3 nights. .Just to give Becks what Posh couldn't give him..

 Senga had also shouted to Posh that at least she's got Tits….

*"No' like you ya' fuckin' pipe cleaner"* Senga had shouted .*"Silicone Sally"*  Senga had called Posh and laughed. *'Hey ! Silicone Sally ! "*   Senga had shouted…*'"Ask David if ma tits are real or no'*?  And big Senga had laughed…And so had the rest of Paterson Park..

To tell you the truth. .It was only because Becks had told the police he was a willing participant that saved Big Senga from the Pokey..

He admitted he'd entered Senga's Mansion of his own free will. .

On Big Senga's pretence of the filter system on her indoor swimming pool not working right....

He admitted to having the obligatory cup of coffee before starting. .Yes..

He told the Police that one thing had led to another....

He'd slipped the Haund first.. Big Senga was innocent of all charges being laid against her....Yes ..Becks had slipped the Haund first..

But he didn't mention that. .Unknown to him. .Big Senga had slipped some date rape drug into his drink.. Twenty minutes after his first mouth-full.. He'd felt awful drowsy...Terribly Drowsy.. The next thing he knew...He'd woke up handcuffed to Big Senga's bed. .

Whereupon.. He'd gladly. .And without any persuading whatsoever...He'd stayed for 3 whole days and 3 whole nights...Honestly officer he'd said. .Honestly..

And the strange thing about this whole carry on.. Was.. Posh seemed to be the only one who was complaining ??
As per usual. Posh was the only one without a smile on their face... Imagine that..??

*The "Senga –Gate Affair" was 3 years ago now…And every Xmas since. .Big S receives a Xmas card signed simply.. To S. .Merry Xmas …Bx.*

But we'll get back to the story now though… Beyoncé has just told the Gals that Calvin was a big advocate of Girl Power…

*''Aw that's braw then''* Madge says.. *''That's braw''*.. But she didn't mean *''That's braw''* in the least….You know Madge yourself by this time and you'll know exactly what she's meaning.. And it's not..  .."That's Braw". .Is it ?...Naw..Is it hell…More like.   .Oh that's braw that your last shite was a Hedgehog…And I pray to God your next one's two Hedgehogs..

Beyoncé also knew Madge didn't mean *''That's Braw''* either. She was pushing all Madge's buttons.. And she'd keep pushing them ….Wasn't Madge trying to nail her to the floor just a wee while ago.. So fuckin' right Beyoncé would keep pushing Madge's buttons. .

So she says

*''Aye it is braw. .It is braw indeed..* An' *Look at aw the braw places he took me to eat ''* She passes her phone back to Rita…Explaining the photo had been taken in

174

Gordon Ramsey's Noo Restaurant in the Brooklyn district of Noo Yoyk.....

Beyoncé was remembering full well how the pair had laughed about Robbie taking her to MacDonald's for a slap up meal...Aye well.. Like she was thinking just a wee while ago.. They deserve to get their noses rubbed right in it..

Rita looked at the screen.. Sure enough there was the bold Beyoncé standing in between Calvin and Gordon Ramsey.. Their arms around each other like they were the very best of pals...It looked like somebody had just told a great joke. .Because they were all genuinely laughing...

*By this time Rita was truly wishing Beyoncé and her really were the very best of pals..*

Rita had never thought she would like to cowp Gordon Ramsey..

Everybody knew he was a big wild Hunk of a Skatsman..

But as Rita for wanting to cowp him..????? ..He had never featured in her sexual fantasies at all.....

Not even in a cameo role..

However ??

However ??.

The size of the bulge in his kilt might convince her otherwise?. .

Maybe .? ..

In fact.. She had already changed her mind..Sha Hoor Sir
.Aye..
Gordon might just be making a cameo appearance tonight
.??....
She could bet there was a lot more than a quarter pound
of prime Skattish beef hanging there alright. .Yum  Yum..
She thought and purred silently to herself......Yum Yum..
Still. .Her and Madge would be getting plenty of that
prime Skattish beef when they came to Leslie. .Wouldn't
they ?..Aye would they.. Plenty..
Beyoncé asks for the phone back again without Madge
even looking at the screen...Rita passes it over.. And
Beyoncé goes through the same rigmarole of tapping and
swiping the screen..

*''There you go Madge''* She says and hands the phone
over.
'

*''That's when Calvin took me to Nick Nairn's new*
*restaurant up in Harlem.*
*.See''* She tells them

Madge takes the phone.. She looks at the screen.. And
sure enough, there's Beyoncé... Nick Nairn and Calvin all
sitting smiling at a posh table laden with all sorts of
culinary delights......Nick's wearing his chefs whites and

Madge thought the meal sitting on the table had been especially cooked for the pair by Nick himself..

Beyoncé tells Madge to swipe on to the next photo.. She does.. She looks at the screen.. She looks at Beyoncé..

*"Is that you wi' Margaret Devine ? "* She enquires.

Beyoncé..She nods ...
*"Yep"* She agrees. .*"It is indeed ..Calvin's took me tae some braw places eh?"*.
Madge doesn't say a word...She just passes the phone over to Rita..
The screen did indeed show Beyoncé and Calvin standing with Margaret Devine.. Margaret was the current owner of the world famous *"Devine's Cake And Coffee Emporium"* ...The shop was first opened in 1873 by Skattish Emigrants and Margaret was the 5th Generation of *"Devine's"* to own the shop.....Noo Yoyk had grown up around Devine's Cake and Coffee Emporium... .And apart from *"Devine's"* being a haunt of all Ex Pat Skatsmen. It was also one of very first must go places for any Skatsmen visiting Noo Yoyk....A Home from Home they say..
Although the Coffee was imported direct from all the great Coffee producing countries in the world.. Columbia. .Brazil.. Peru.Etc..Etc.. The Tea was imported direct from Skatland.... Loose tea.. Tea leaves...It was the only place in

Noo Yoyk you could by traditional Skattish cake. .Dundee Cake ..Black Bun and all the rest of it... ...You could also buy genuine Traditional Tunnock's Tea Cakes..Tunnock's Caramel wafers.. You could by a Dundee Peh...You could buy Walkers traditional Scottish shortbread.. Lees macaroon bars...A traditional Forfar Bridie.. And glass bottles of Irn-Bru..Then.. Of course.. There was also the home baking..."Love At First Bite".. As a visiting Poet had once described Margaret's homemade.. Victoria Sponge.....''If you're stressed'' The poet had written..

*If you're stressed... Or fell depressed...*
*If you feel your hearts and heads are messed....*
*You'll truly feel like you've been blessed....*
*When first you step into Devine's..*

Then he'd went on to write verse upon verse about the delights of Margaret's homemade cakes..   Especially her Victoria sponge..

*You can eat it till your heart's content''..* The Poet had wrote.
*You can eat it till your money's spent''..*

A lovely poem altogether.  .But sure ..You can read the whole poem for yourself when you visit Devine's , as Margaret has it  framed and hanging on her wall..

Amongst the photos of all the past stars of Movies and Music world, who always paid them a visit...Humphrey Bogart.. Frank Sinatra.  Clint Eastwood. .All the members of Runrig   Steve Harley and his band.. Cockney Rebel. Sean Connery. Billy Connolly. Etc..Etc..
And more recently... The Selfies taken with the modern day stars.
. And soon..
 Another photo would be appearing on the wall in Devine's soon as well..
One of Calvin and his new found sweetheart.. The love of his life...Beyoncé....


Margaret had told them that ''*Amy*'' her oldest daughter was returning back to the family roots soon .And opening the families first cake And Coffee Emporium in Bonnie Skatland.....Leslie to be exact....And Calvin has agreed to open it when the time comes.. Calvin's got a Mansion there she tell the pair.. In Paradise Park she boasts.....But.... As we all know, Paradise Park is only the name the Paparazzi call it because of the pure opulence of the street..
It's the only street in Skatland ..In fact...It's the only place in Skatland where Orange Trees.. Coconut Trees.. Palm trees and Mango Trees line the pavements... And of course. .Of course... It's called Paradise Park after the pure class of the people who live there...Or have ever.. Ever

had the honour of gracing these most hallowed of pavements.... And there has been a lot of them...And a lot more wish they had a connection to this street.. Any connection whatsoever..

That most famous of streets indeed...Indeed. You've heard it mentioned a few times over the course of the story

It's really called Paterson Park ..And If you had an address in Paterson Park. .Then.. Jesus. .It didn't half open some doors for you in this life I'll tell you...

If you had the Postcode K.Y.6 3.D.X.?....Then that told the whole wide world many things about you......One of them was that you were loaded with cash.. Loaded.....More money than a Horse could shite..

And that's the very street where Big Senga had kidnaped David Beckham...Remember I mentioned it a wee while ago?...3 whole days.. And 3 whole nights Big Senga had held him captive....
That had been the end of the line for Posh though. .And as it turned out. .It was also the end of David's short lived career with Leslie Hearts... ..It didn't take ''*The Paparazzi*'' long to get hold of the story though.... ..And of course, all the other Gals around town were desperate to get all the

Goss from Big Senga...Asking all the stories about her 3 day adventure with Becks

*''What size was his cock Senga ''*? Kelly Robb asked

Alexis Sweeney was desperate to find out. *''Is his cock as big as they say it is Senga?*

*''Was Becks a good ride Senga''* ? All the Gals were wanting to know.

Asking all the questions Gals ask each other about their latest click..
And Big Senga had indeed got a click eh?   ...
But Senga had just smiled.. And wouldn't tell the Paparazzi anything. ..
Neither would anybody else in Paterson Park..
The Paparazzi were told kindly to *''Get Themselves To Fuck''* when they went knocking on the peoples doors.....Leaving everybody in the whole wide world guessing....
So as usual.....The Paparazzi just used their fertile imaginations to make up the rest of the story for what was to become *''The Senga Gate Affair''*.. And  it also left all Big Senga's pals none the wiser to the question they had asked her over and over....

*"Did you make Becks take you up ?.. You know"?...Did you Senga" Did you ???'." Did he" ? .*
Maybe you also know the question they weren't getting an answer to..

But like I was saying. .If I've got the time ..I'll tell you more about it later on. It all depends....We'll just have to wait and see..

Anyway.. The sight of all that delicious food in Gordon Ramsey's and Nick Nairn's...And the very thought of all the lovely choice of cakes in Devine's had brought on *"The Munchies"* even worse for Madge..

You already know they had both took a terrible attack before Beyoncé had even arrived on the scene. And how long was that ago now?. .You know how Madge had cancelled making that lovely Italian dish until Beyoncé had done the bunk.. But now.. With sitting smoking all that weed.. She really was gutting...And she knew fine Rita would be feeling the same way..
She felt like asking Beyoncé if she fancied staying for tea? ...She did. .That's how starving she was.. But then again? . .She thought to herself.. Then again.? . That Hoor would just think Madge was trying to crawl up her arse.. And Madge wouldn't want her to think that....And another reason was. .It would mean another Hour.. Maybe an

Hour and a Half of listening to Beyoncé blaw.. Blaw..
Fuckin' Blaw about her sexual conquests...And stuff that.
Beyoncé was nothing but a Hoor......
She should be ashamed of herself.. Not that Madonna
was jealous or anything … Oh No..Never..Gawd..Her and
Beyoncé were pals for Christ's sake..

Then Beyoncé tells them it was while sitting in ;*"Devine's"*
Calvin's asked her if she would consider doing a  Duet
with him on his next record..?..

And Madonna nearly fainted..

*''What did you say''* Asked Rita.. Sounding like she really
was interested.

And Madonna just glowered her.. She was supposed to be
Madge's best pal isn't she ?.

But Beyoncé replies that she'd nearly bit the fuckin' hand
off him at the offer.
All her nearest and dearest dreams had come true she
tells them.   .All her prayers had been answered.....In the
space of less than a fortnight

*"Oh that's jist great.. Ye' jist never know what 's roond the
next corner eh no' ''* ? Rita asked ..Hoping Madge would

fall out with her....Cause.. Well.. She wouldn't mind being Rita's pal now..

Beyoncé..She tells them she's already made up a song..

*''What is it aboot''* ? Asked Rita.

Beyoncé..She replies by sticking her tongue out and waving it about.. Just like she's performing oral sex on another woman...

*If you're perhaps copying Beyoncé sticking her tongue out? ...The same as you did earlier on with Madonna licking the saucer-full of milk? Then please remember Beyoncé has her tongue out and is wriggling about for nearly 4 seconds....Try it again if you wish. That's it .Stick your tongue right out and wriggle it about like you're performing Oral sex on a woman...That's it. .Perfect.. Spot on.. Now wriggle it about...4..3..2..1...And back in again. .That's it. .Perfect...*

*A wee word of warning though.. Please be careful if you're reading this book on a train or a plane....Because you're guaranteed to get some funny looks.*
*.If. .However. .You're in a Doctors waiting room.. Or in a Hospital?...Then please don't even try it..*

.''What's that''?  Asks Rita. .Sticking her own tongue out and copying Beyoncé..
4.3.2.1.  That's it.. You've got it spot on. .Perfect.. And back in again.

''Connie Lingiss''   Beyoncé explains

''Connie who ?''   Rita enquires..

Beyoncé tells Rita it's not Connie anybody.. It's 'Connie Lingiss'' she says...
''Ah'v not a fuckin' clue how tae spell it'' she explains.
.''But that's what it's called. ''Connie Lingiss''...The art of performing Oral sex on a woman...Muff Divin'' in other words..

''You're writin' a song aboot Muff Divin''' ? Rita gasps..
''Are ye' really ?''

''What's wrang wi' that''?  Beyoncé asks. .''You like getting' ye'r pussy kissed dae ye' no'?

Rita had to agree.. Oh aye..Yum..Yum. .She loved getting her pussy kissed. Loved it..Fuckin' absolutely loved it.. In fact. .It was only just last night. .Late on...After another day of smoking weed and dreaming about all the big time stars of the music and Movie world her and Madge were going to ride when they were on their big adventure to Skatland.. She'd been fantasising about Dougray Scott kissing her pussy. .While she'd been wanking off Gerard Butler and Daniel Craig at the same time.. Then they'd all swapped places.. And Gerard had begun to caress her clitty with his tongue..

Madge loved getting her pussy kissed as well. .Oh Sha Hoor.. She didnae half…..
Her problem was the same as many woman's problems when it came to Muff Diving…  It was very difficult to find a guy who could do it right…
A lot of Guys thought they could. .But then again. A lot of Guys thought their cocks were massive..

And what Rita or Beyoncé didn't know ..Was ..Last night. .Late on. .After another day spent smoking weed and searching through all the Leslie guys Facebook pages…Madge had been fantasising about the very same thing as Rita…
It had only started out as a wee pat or two, if you know what I mean?..  Honestly…It was just supposed to be a wee friendly reassuring pat or two of her pussy .Just thinking about all the famous Movie stars they were going to meet in Skatland… …Then.. It had quickly turned into the thousand rubs.. And in last night's fantasy.. She'd been thrusting her pussy down on Calvin Harris's face.

Thrusting it down.. Just like you're picturing...She would have loved to have screamed with pleasure.. But in this fantasy. .Her mouth had been full. .And you know what it had been full of don't you.? .Gerard Butlers if you must know. .Both her hands had been kept busy as well.... Doing just exactly what you're imagining she was doing.. Then everybody had swapped places...... But that was last night. .And as you'll have noticed Madge isn't saying much at all right now... .She's being awfy quiet.. As quite as a Church mouse..

Rita tells Beyoncé there's nothing wrong with writing a song about Muff Diving. .Oh no...Nothing wrong at all with that.. She says it's a great thing for somebody to write a song about...A magical thing....Then she explains the reason she had sounded so surprised was that she's never heard a song about that particular subject before. .Never. And she was a huge music fan..

Beyoncé tells Rita she's already written the song, and all it needs now is for Calvin to mix some music to go with the words....She reaches into her M.K. Handbag again.. She brings out a crumpled up bit paper.. Which she flattens out on the coffee table.... Then she asks if Rita wants to hear the song. ? .
 Without waiting on an answer. .She gets up out the chair.
.

She wriggles that sweet ass about…Just exactly like you're imagining….Imitating Both Madge and Rita a wee while ago.
Remember when they were spouting the pish they'd wrote.?.

Beyoncé tells the pair this is only the first draft of the Muff Diving song…

*''We'll have to tweak it a bit'' She explains.'' Maybe include another verse ''*

Then ..Reading from the uncrumpled bit paper… She starts singing loudly..

*''It drives me tae Insanity''*. She sung loudly and she lifts up her leopard skin mini skirt.. Then she grabs her Toosh.. She's thrusting her hips forward…
Look at her there.. Just look at her……

And she's still singing the world's first ever Muff Diving song…

*''It drives me tae Insanity,
Cause ah just can't get enough.
Ah don't care aboot ma vanity..
Ah love ma love tae kiss ma Fluff..*

188

She lets go her Toosh ..Her mini skirt slips back into place...

Then she sung what she said was the chorus..

*"So come Guys or Gals... Rip aff ma Kegs.'..*
*And ram ye'r heed between ma legs.*
*Oh let your tongue explore ma pussy.*
*Make ma Piss flaps braw an' juicy..*
*Give me what i want.. What i really ..Really want. "*

Then she told them this was the second verse.. And she continued singing...

*Oh kiss ma slit. .Oh lick ma clit.....*
*That's one thing you can't deny me.*
*Let your tongue caress ma favourite bit..*
*Until you satisfy me".*

Then it was back to the chorus ..Can you hear Rita singing along with Beyoncé..?...

*"Give me what I want.. What I really.. Really want..".*.

Then Beyoncé. .She grabs her Toosh again....Then she shakes her whole body a good bit. ..Shaking.. Shaking. .Shaking. .Just like you're imagining..

Her legs are shaking like she's dancing to an Elvis Presley song...Can you see her there ? Imitating she is really is climaxing with somebody kissing her Toosh....
Then sits back down again...
*''What dae ye' hink oh that song then Ree*? She asked

*''Oh that's a brilliant song B''*.. Rita answered..*'' Fantastic, It really is. .The world's first song aboot Muff Divin'..It's bound tae be a huge Massive hit.. Bound tae be...,Bound to be.''*

Already.. *''The Muff Diving song''* Was becoming an earworm for Rita.. But then again. .Didn't she fancy being the backing singer?  . .
But like all earworms. .They get very annoying..

*''It drives me tae Insanity''*   She was hearing over and over and over and over again in her imagination.......

*'Cause ah just can't get enough''*

I hope *''The Muff Diving ''*Song isn't becoming an earworm for you as well??

*''Ah don't care aboot ma vanity*
*Ah love ma love tae kiss ma fluff.*

If it is.? .Then don't forget the chorus..

*"So come Guys Or Gals. Rip aff Ma Kegs.*
*An' ram ye'r heed between ma legs".*

And here.. Another thing. .If Beyoncé and Calvin.. With
the world's first ever song about *''Muff Diving''* does
make it into the charts ?..Then you can have the honour
of saying you were amongst the first to ever hear it..  Even
before it was tweaked up and had maybe another verse
added.....
 In fact. You'll be amongst the very first to ever have sung
it.. Cause I have the feeling you'll have sung it a few times
by now.. .

And I hope you haven't been singing it aloud on the Plane
or a Train or that Mind you ..It would be funny .It would
be....Do you fancy it ?.....Just for a right good laugh...If you
are on a Plane or a Train? . .The folk next to you will
already have been giving you funny looks when you've
been sticking your tongue out.. When you were imitating
Madge with the saucer-full of milk... And when you've
been copying Beyoncé performing Oral sex on a
woman...So imagine the looks on their faces when you
burst into ... *''The Muff Diving Song ''* ?
These folk will never see you in their lives again anyway.
.C'mon. .Just say a big boy made you do it. C'Mon...Just

for a laugh... What's the worst that could happen ?.......Let's burst into *''The Muff Diving Song''*..
Sing like you're trying your hardest to get in the church choir..
 I'll start.. You join in. .Sing it Loud And Sing it Proud..

*''It drives me tae insanity.*
*Cause ah just can't get enough''*

That's it...Well done....I didn't realise you were such a good singer.. Keep going through....But Louder.!!

*''Ah don't care aboot ma vanity.*
*Ah love ma love tae kiss ma fluff''*

I'll not write the chorus down again.. Just to see if you can remember it.

Have a wee quick squint and see the funny looks now. Because you'll be getting plenty...... Then start on the second verse..... .Surely you can remember that as well.. ?...Have a look now...See if anybody's on the phone to security ?..Or the Doctor..?  ..If They do arrive on the scene? ..Just show them this...Just to prove you're not Mad after all..

Beyoncé explains Calvin's not sure whether to do a bit of Rapping with this song or not?

They had discussed doing a version with just electronic music. .

They had even talked about doing a Reggae version .

Calvin had even dreamed about doing a true Skattish version of the Muff Diving song... With the haunting sound of the Bagpipes .Flutes.. .Bohdrans.. .The Full Monty.

*At this point Ladies And Gentlemen. .You might like to go and read the world's first ever '' Muff Diving Song'' All over again...And choose for yourself what version you fancy the best.*

*It might sound better if you read it with a wee tune in mind..,,*

*See if you fancy a Reggae Version ?.Bob Marley or U.B.40. Styllee Man..*

*Or maybe you hear it more as a Rave song..? .Rub a Dub style... With all the scratching...You know.?   All those ''Ccchhhgggss''..And'' Ccchhaaaggs'' dubbed over the words..*

*Maybe you even feel Pink Floyd would make a good job of it ?*

*Or perhaps you hear it best as Country And Western number.? ..*

*Maybe like something Johnny Cash would sing ?  .....*

*Or do you hear The Skattish version ?   With the haunting
sound of the Bagpipes and the Flutes etc, playing over the
top of Beyoncé singing . ..*
*It's entirely up to yourself?. .*
*Cause it's only in your own imagination anyway..  What
one do you fancy the very best ?*

And all the time, Rita was thinking.  .If only I could get
Madge to fall out with me.?   Then I could be Beez bestest
pal for evermore.. And maybe I'll ask if she could have a
wee word in Calvin's ear. ?  .Maybe ask if he needs a
backing singer on his latest hit…. The world's first ever
song about Muff Diving..?
Gawd ..She was even imagining herself doing the filthy
moaning on the song. Like on that Old French song they
used to play at the end of the Discos...At the Erection
Section .*"Je Temme"* it's called ..If she remembers
correctly..

Without being asked Madge said Beyoncé's song was
shite..
That's what she was saying. .But she was thinking a
different thing altogether.. She was thinking…. If only I
could remember the words of *"The Muff Diving Song"*.
??...Rita and me could maybe add another verse of our
own and record it ourselves using some of that lovely cash
from Barry Bang,,Bang.?.. We could get right in there. ..

.Long before that Hoor Beyoncé and Calvin even got the chance...They could put it on You-tube music. .Gawd..Even the title would encourage people to download it. .The world's first song about Muff Diving.. They'd make a fortune. .An absolute fortune...But she couldn't remember the words... She's already told Beyoncé her song's shite. .So she couldn't exactly ask her to repeat the words. .Could she ?.

*"A lot oh utter shite "* She says .Then she asked who the fuck would want to listen to a song about Muff Diving ?

*"Every Gal in the world "* Beyoncé replies. ."Calvin says *it'll be an anthem for all the frustrated Gals who love getting their Pussies kissed"*... Then she tells them...
*"Calvin says these kinda Gals will play it over and over and over again.. Hoping their man will get the hint...*
*"Anyway"* She tells Madge..*" "Ma song's a lot better that pish you wrote"*.

*"Oh dae ye' think so"*? Madge answered. ."*Dae ye'hink so"*?

*"Aye ah do hink so"* Beyoncé laughed. ."*In fact a ken so"* She tells them. ..
*"Calvin says Oor song will be a Shooge.. Shooge... Massive hit amongst the Lesbian community anaw...'..*Then she

looks directly at Madge .And she says. .*"After all Madge. Only another woman really knows where to find the Zones Eh"?*

Madge.. She drops her eyes double quick.. ..Then just let out a *"Humph"* in way of a reply..
And Beyoncé continues.. Continues driving the nails in. . Well Madge needn't think she was nailing the Beyoncé one to the floor..

She tells the pair that Calvin says the likes of his pal… Horse McDonald, will be singing the Muff Diving song at the start of the Gay Pride marches an' awhing..

Rita always thought *"Horse"* was as rather strange name for a Lesbian to have as a nickname.. Because.. Well… Every time she heard somebody with the nickname *"Horse"*.. Only one image sprung to her mind. .Then again. .Maybe that's just Rita. ?..And the image wasn't of a big butch Lesbian. .I can tell you that much..
And every time she heard of somebody with that Nickname.. She hoped it wasn't because he had a fondness for sugar lumps. .*"Horse"* ? Sha..Hoor..Sir. Let me in aboot them..

Beyoncé remembered she had told Calvin that Kunda Saharan would be proud of a song like they'd just written... .She was trying to be all intellectual and impress Calvin with her knowledge of literature...She didn't think he would have ever heard of Kunda before. .But he'd agreed.  .He did. .Calvin knew all about Kunda. .He'd read Dessie's ''CUNT''  as well.....And just like you....He had ordered a few copies off Amazon for his loved ones Birthdays and Xmas........Imagine that eh ??

But Beyoncé gets all dreamy like. She's got that star struck look in her eyes and she says...''Me an' Calvin''
.''Calvin an Me... Jist imagine it Gals'' She says......
Top Of The Pops ..Here we come'' She says.....''We'll be on the Rollaine Kelly show an awhing. .....

Beyoncé's got a bit mixed up ..Saying things like a Dyslexic would see them on the page... .It's the weed.. But I'm sure you know who she means eh?.. Yeah...That's right. .Lorraine Kelly.....The beautiful Lorraine.. Everybody's favourite T.V. Presenter.....And a proud Skatswoman as well..

' We'll be on the Rollaine Kelly show an'
awhing...Worldwide fame and fortune'' She says..
.''Everybody will be jealous of me'.. ''Everybody'' !!  She repeats and smiles over at Madge.

Madge smiles back.. With the kind of smile that would look just perfect on a Crocodile..

Beyoncé knew what was coming next. .
And so should you. .
You've been sitting paying attention for a good wee while now and you can't have failed to pick up on the atmosphere..
But Beyoncé knew fine what would happen when she told them the next bit..
The bit she'd been dying to tell them..
So she does.

*"Calvin's recording studio's under his Mansion in Paterson Park"* She looks at Madge and smiles widely and repeats *"Paterson Park. .Leslie  Skatland"*..
She lets on she's getting all starry eyed. .Like she's trying to impress Simon Cowall...Then she almost shouts....
*"*Ah'm goin' *tae Skatland Madge  ..Skatland"*..

And Madge losses the plot. .She does….. Losses it altogether…
Just like Beyoncé knew she would..
And probably just like you had guessed as well..
And Rita was glad…

Did you notice how quick Madge jumped up out her chair there?
Sha..Hoor.Sir. .That was fast.. ......You'd have thought the Polis were at the door........?.

''*See you ya' Caant* '' She points at Beyoncé and she's shouting...

That was one of the words neither of the two Gals could do in a Skattish accent..''*Caant*''...But I'm sure you know what Madge means eh ?  ''*Caant.*''

''*See you ya caant*'' Madge is shouting.. *''Is that aw ye' got that Helicopter tae drap ye' aff here fir Eh..Jist tae rub oor fuckin; Noses in it ?..Tryin' tae make us fuckin' jealous eh?'*

Rita  ..She's hoping for a fight this time. .She is.. She's hoping for a right set two between the pair.. And it wouldn't be the first time either..
You already know what they're like with each other sometimes.....Oh aye. They'd had some cracking fights the pair of them. .Like cat and dog...
And sometimes Rita thought Madge had a wee bit of a hard neck calling Beyoncé a Psycho....Cause.. Well...Look at her now for instance?..

While Beyoncé?. .She's still sitting smiling at Madge....She's very serene.... Even though she's on the weed, this isn't like her...
She shouldn't be letting Madge shout at her like that. .
It's not what we were expecting.. Eh no?
It's certainly not what Rita was expecting ..
And it's not what she was wanting either...
You've already seen them at each other's throats earlier on..
So do they go for it this time?.. Just wait and see..

 Beyoncé might be sitting there looking like the epitome of serenity,  She might be thinking ''*Sticks and Stones Madge Doll.. Sticks and Stones.*'' but she's also thinking. ''.*Take two steps closer ya Hoor..Two steps closer and ah'll lift ma leg so fast...I'll bury ma high heel that far up ye'r Hole it'll knock ye'r teeth oot*''...

Madge doesn't step forward though, but she's still ranting on...Telling Beyoncé she should be ashamed of herself...Ashamed of filming herself rodgering all these men. .Some of them are married she was shouting.. She told Beyoncé she had no respect for herself.....( *Imagine Madge telling folk they should respect themselves eh* ? ) .She was asking Beyoncé if she had ever thought of all the trouble it would cause if any of these Dudes wife's ever get a hold of the video.?

''Ah Ha'' Thought Beyoncé....''Here we go...Here we fuckin' go...Madge is trying to wheedle me into a Scam''.. But she's also thinking..''Sha..Hoor..Sir.. That's the pot calling the kettle black...It really is''.. Because Beyoncé could rattle off at least a half a dozen married men that Madge had cowped..And that was only in the 3 years they'd known each other...

She's letting Madge's ranting wash off her like water off a ducks back..

She knows fine its jealousy and frustration dressed up as anger...

And she's thinking. .''Cool The Beans Madge Doll.....Calm Hen. .Calm. .Mellow Madge.... Mellow.''

And she's also thinking .''Instead of This Skitzo Hoor planning to go to Skatland..She really should go to the Andie Mountains to learn Meditating'. .Mellow Madge Doll. .Mellow.''.

But Madge doesn't have her Yoga head on.. She's not interested in Buddha.. She's not interested in hearing wee cymbals being tapped together gently or Pan Pipes.... Not tonight Josephine.. ..She's still on about Beyoncé being nothing but a Hoor and all the rest of it  .But as you know .It's all just going right over Beyoncé's head.....

While Beyoncé.. She's thinking .."*You've had your wings clipped Madge Doll.. But if you just wait a wee minute hen... You'll be feeling like an ostrich.. You'll not be able to fly at all."*......

She's waiting on Madge burning herself out before she tells her though...
But then again. .Madge might just try to Lowp on top of her..
 Beyoncé was ready for that though. .She'd lift her leg so fast. .That..

And Rita.? .Well...Rita's sitting sooking on her Grass joint and she's thinking..."*Goan Madge....Goan....Lowp right on top of her. .Try and skart her Een oot...Goan Madge*"

She's only thinking that...Because Madge and her are best pals aren't they ? But if Madge would just lowp on top of Beyoncé.?   .Well. .Maybe things would change?  Maybe ?...

She still couldn't get that fuckin' Muff Diving song out her head either...It was The Reggae version she was hearing now. ..Maybe you can imagine that version as well ?...Try and Imagine Bob Marley or U.B.40 singing it..

*"It drives me tae Insanity"*

*Cause ah just can't get enough"..*

That's what her earworm was singing again. .Over and over and over....

*"Ah don't care aboot ma vanity..*
*Ah love ma love tae kiss ma fluff"*

Rita's also thinking that if these pair do start fighting then at least it won't be her flat they're wrecking this time.. Because a few times in the past.? . Fuck sake... There was one time. .About a month ago...They were all in Rita's flat when the pair been going Ding-Dong at each other.. It was while *"The Chase"* was on the Telly funnily enough...Beyoncé had answered a lot more questions than the pair of them .But Madge had lost the head altogether and chucked a plate at Beyoncé ..But Beyoncé had quickly ducked out the road.. The Tapas dish Rita had cooked for dinner landed all over the living room carpet..... .But the plate had crashed right through Rita's living room window. .

*You should have heard the rumours the Roving Reporter invented about that incident. .She still doesn't know the right story though..*

Still.. Even that didn't turn out all bad. .Because Rita and Madge had both cowped Kevin White, the council joiner, when he'd came to replace the window.

.*"Every cloud's got a silver lining"* Madge had told Rita after Kevin had left...

*'It's an ill wind that blows nobody any good Rita Doll"*

It doesn't seem like Madge is getting the response she wanted from Beyoncé ..In fact.. She's not getting any reaction at all….It's either that or she has burnt herself out at last.. …Because that a wee while she's been ranting on now eh ?..A good 5 minutes anyway eh ?.

Madge turns round.. And Beyoncé waits until she's flopped her arse back down on her chair before speaking..

The first thing Rita does is pass Madge the joint..

*"Do ye' really think ?"* Beyoncé asked …*"Dae ye' really think ah got Floyd tae drop me off here jist tae rub ye'r noses in it ?..Dae ye ?"*

*"Aye we do "* Madge stated.

''Aye.. Well. .That's where ye'r wrang'' Beyoncé replied.
''Cause that's no' the reason''

''Aye it fuckin' is'' Madge snapped.. ''Jist tae rub oor noses
in it.. Eh Rita''?

Now Rita. .She didn't know how to answer. .
She felt caught between the Devil and the deep blue sea..

She could say.. ''Aye Madge.. That's all she done it for
Madge.. Just tae rub oor noses right in it''.

She could say...''Ye'r right enough Madge. .Beyoncé is jist
nothin' but a slapper....She'd no right putting her knickers
back on. .Rubbing our noses in it.. Cause we know the
reason she had them off in the first place'''..

Or she could say. .''Aye Madge. Ye'r right Madge...If any
of these Dudes wife's ever see that video ? ..It'll cause a
Hoor oh a bother. .A Hoor oh a bother !! .''   .

Oh aye...Rita could stir the shite even further. Try and get
Madge to lowp right on top of Beyoncé...Then Rita could
separate the pair..
 Maybe she could take Beyoncé's side..??..
Shout all the things you shout when you're trying to stop
your two best pals tearing lumps out each other.??.

*"Moan Tae Fuck an' behave yersel's ya daft pair oh Cannts"*..Things like that..
Make Beyoncé think she had come to her rescue ??

She didn't want to take Beyoncé's side and risk upsetting Madge though....

But then again.. She didn't want to risk upsetting Beyoncé either... And you know all the reasons why don't you ?.... Being Beez pal might mean an introduction to Calvin..???...Then..?  Maybe a wee turn as a backing singer on that song that was still playing over and over and over in her mind..?. .It was The Skattish version she was hearing this time.. With the haunting sound of the Bagpipes etc....

*"It drives me tae Insanity.*
*Cause ah jist can't get enough"*

Being a friend of Calvin's also brought along all these other added benefits.. As you've just seen on the video..Gawd... Rita had to stop herself from imagining herself and Calvin swimming bare naked in his swimming pool. .In his Mansion. In Paterson Park.. With Dougray Scott and Gerard Butler swanning about naked as the day they were born, serving cocktails......

Then later on they would both be telling her Cock-Tales
???

"O.M.G" ..She was thinking silently.. *"Oh ! My ! Fuckin'*
*!.God !"*... .Imagine Rita being able to boast to everybody
that she had been to Paterson Park. Leslie. .Fife.
?...Paterson Park ??

Everybody would want to know her then eh ?..Aye would
they...

Then if course.. If all this were to come true ?..That would
mean moving out of Hollywood .Out the clutches of Barry
Bang  Bang and his even crazier band of sisters
altogether...That in itself would be a positive lifestyle
choice.....

She didn't really fancy growing weed in her attic for the
rest of her life..   But  hadn't Barry easily convinced her
and Madge they were onto a sure fire winner.. All that
cash.. Right on the nose.. Every 3
months..Lovely..Jubbley..And Madge had agreed with
him. .Lovely Jubbley


*And of course.. Wasn't it Madge who convinced Rita not
to have anything to do with P.O.F or any of these other
dating websites ?..Gawd..If she'd only listened to
Beyoncé??..Rita could maybe have been away down to
Noo Yoyk with her.... She had to secretly admire the
Beyoncé one for having the balls to go away all that
distance on her own in the first place. .*

*And look what had happened to her eh ?..Aye .Just look what had happened to her ..Rita wasn't jealous though .Well ...Not as Jealous as Madge was anyway..*

And the thing is. .With Madge being such a master at the scamming. .Rita thought she would have cottoned onto all this as well...
Cottoned on to the fact that it would be better to keep on Beyoncé's good side.
Knowing Madge as we do...Maybe she did have something up her sleeve ?

Rita had also had to be very careful not to think too loud...
Because of that Telepathy I was telling you about earlier on......
So she's being extra careful not to think.. If only ?...If only..
And if only she could get that *''Muff Diving Song ''* Out her head as well....
She was back to hearing the Reggae version again...Bob Marley style..

*''So come Guys or Gals Rip Aff Ma Kegs.*
*An' Ram Ye'r Heed Between Ma Legs''*

So to keep the peace. ..Although it wouldn't keep the peace one bit.. She told Madge that maybe Beyoncé didn't get dropped off in the Helicopter just to rub their noses in it.. Maybe there was another reason she states.. ...But that's as much as she got to say because Madge starts shouting at her. She does. .She's shouting there's no other reason Beyoncé got dropped off outside their homes in the Helicopter. .No other reason.. Just to rub their noses right in it,...

Rita's thinking..Sha Hoor  Sir.. Keep shoutin' Madge. .Just you keep shoutin' doll. .Because all this might just turn out in my favour .. Cause I'll not put up with any of your pish either......I might get the chance to fall out with you after all Madge....

She's also thinking.. *"The Chase"* Will have finished by this time.. Madge had won last night and Rita was desperate to get her own back tonight....But the real live Drama unfolding before her eyes was much more fun.. As you know.. Rita had to be extremely careful not to think too loud though...Just in case Madge heard her,....

So. .Just to wind Madge up even more.. She tells her the worst thing you can ever.. Ever say to anybody who's wound right up to 99...
She tells her to calm down and not to get her knickers in a twist...And of course that had the opposite effect. .Madge

pushes herself halfway up out her chair. .Look at Madge..
Can you see her there ?..

Who the hell is she trying to kid on she's not jealous, Eh
?...
You heard Madge yourself.. Earlier on there.... Singing
these songs she made up about the amount of shagging
her and Rita planned to do when they were in Leslie..
 They were going to cowp all the Leslie Guys weren't they
?
You also know all about her fantasies involving the Dudes
from Leslie Hearts and Lad--Zone.. So she's not kidding
anybody.

Listen to her shouting at Rita that she's not fuckin'
needing to calm down and she's not getting her knickers
in a twist either. .She's also going on again about how
Beyoncé is nothing but a Hoor..She should be ashamed of
herself she shouts.. Then she sits back down again....

Rita's not sure if Madge has noticed Beyoncé raking in her
M.K. Handbag again because she's still on about how
she's ashamed to say that she's a friend of a Hoor like
that..   Then she goes on about all the trouble it could
cause with all these Guys wife's if they were ever to see
the photos or that fuckin' disgusting Video..

Beyoncé interrupts Madge's tirade when she slaps an Envelope down on the table...A Brown Envelope it is......A biggish Envelope. .Not A4 size.. Maybe A5 ? What do you think ?....The Envelope's lying on its face so Rita couldn't see if it has an address on it or not ?.....Did you manage to get a quick squint from where you're sitting ?.. In any case ..It lands with a *'Thump''* ..And Madge stops ranting..

It's Beyoncé who's doing all the talking now...She's still swiping through her phone and she's asking Madge if she would cowp all those famous Movie stars if she had the chance ?

Madge doesn't reply to that particular question.. Everybody knows the answer anyway..

So Beyoncé asks Rita the same thing...And only got a wish-full look as an answer...

Beyoncé asks Madge the same question again.?

*''Even though ah did'* 'Madge barks. .*''Even though ah did cowp them.. Ah certainly widdnae get it videoed fir aw the world tae see''* ...'

.But Beyoncé knows she's a liar...She doesn't say that though...She tells them that the photos were for their eyes only..

She says she wasn't going to show them to another soul. .Just Madge and Rita..."*Jist tae let ma twa best pals ken what wiz in store fir them*". She tells them.. Then she says that's her just deleted all the photos..

Madge goes to say something but Beyoncé holds up her hand.. *'Hold on"* she tells Madge. *."Hold on"*. She's still swiping on her phone...

Madge was more than likely going to ask the same question Rita was just about to ask...What the Hell did Beyoncé mean by. *".Jist tae let ye'r twa best pals ken what's in store fir them"*?.

While Rita ?...Well...She was hoping the two best pals meant her and Madge..

But Beyoncé's just told Madge to hold on....

Then they hear the sound of Beyoncé squealing with pleasure again. .It's the Video.. Rita's hoping ...Well. .She's praying.. Beyoncé is maybe going to let them see it for a second time. .But no   The squealing stopped....Beyoncé tells them the video's deleted as well.. She's telling them nobody else was ever going to see the video either. .''*For your eyes only*'' she tells the pair....

Madge does get a word in eventually.. She asks Beyoncé just what the fuck she meant by ..''*Jist tae let ye'r twa best pals ken what in store*''?

Beyoncé.. She puts her phone down then picks up the Brown Envelope.. ..
She tells them that it doesn't matter a monkeys fuck now..

Madge shouts that Beyoncé couldn't tell them half a story..

Beyoncé replies calmly that she's not telling her half a story.
Rita thinks Beyoncé is getting a wee bit emotional ...Cause her hands are shaking. .Maybe it was just temper?
....Whatever it was.......She's hiding it well though...
Perfectly.....
''*Well.*''' She says.. ''*You two are ma best pals are ye'z no'?.*
She opens the Brown Envelope.... And takes out another Envelope.. A white one this time..
She doesn't open that Envelope though. No.. She just rips it right in half.

Then she rips these half's into half's and keeps ripping
...Her hands are still shaking. .And she's talking like she's
talking to herself.. She's saying that she was a stupid
Caannt for even mentioning that pair to Calvin in the first
place...
 She throws the torn up Envelope on the coffee table.
.They're lying there like a Hundred piece jigsaw..

She is getting emotional...And this is the last thing
Beyoncé expected to happen.. She thought she really
would enjoy nailing Madge and Rita to the floor. .Making
them sick as a pigs....Well it's not her fault that she's a
sensitive Gal...She'll have to pull herself together..
Sharpish...
She wipes her sleeve across her eyes as if to wipe away a
tear.. And she's still talking to herself, saying these two
Cannts never gave her a single thought when they were
making their Holiday plans.. So she was a stupid
mentioning anything about them to Calvin..

It was obvious Madonna wasn't going to ask the
question.. ..So Rita felt like she had to..   And she did
.''What wir ye' sayin' tae Calvin aboot us B ? ''

'''What wiz ah no' sayin''' Beyonce replied. .''Ah telt him
you two were ma best pals in the world.''  She is getting
right in a state now.. Her efforts to pull herself

together...Sharpish.. Weren't working........She lifts her phone again but keeps talking.. *"'Ah telt um ye'z were always there for me"* She says.. *"Anytime.. An' when ah says ah wid maybe get a bit fed up paddin' aboot that big mansion when he's awa' on tour.. He says ma two best pals could maybe come ower an' keep me company.."*....

She presses the screen of her phone a couple of times ,,She holds the phone away a wee bit from her face. .She must have put it on loudspeaker because the other two could hear the ringing tone.. And it rung and it rung ...Then it was answered. .And Beyoncé says..

*"Hello there Calvin. Hooz it hangin'"?*

Then they heard a man answer in a sexy Skattish accent..

*"It's hangin' jist braw doll"* He says.. *"Ye're lookin' fair braw in your sexy new claes there'"*...

Of course Calvin had never seen her in her sexy new claes had he.? .No he hadn't, because he had just given Beyoncé his American Express Gold card and told her to buy some new gear for her trip tae Scotland.......Then Floyd and her had went on a shopping spree around Noo Yoyk before boarding the Helicopter...But just hearing Calvin say these words lifted Beyoncé's spirits just a wee

bit....They couldn't have lifted them enough though..
Because Calvin asks if she's awright...?.. ..And this is how
the rest of the conversation went..

*"Ah'm fine Calvin Ma wee Braveheart"..* Beyoncé replied
*'Ah'm fine"..* And then she sniffed quickly a couple of
times. .The way people who are right upset sniff...

It was then Rita realised Beyoncé was talking on Facetime
...And she's thinking *"Calvin"* ?? Sha Hoor Sir.. That must
be Calvin Harris she's talkin' tae.
And immediately. .Her imagination was forming images of
her. .Rita.. Doing the backing singer on that song.. That
song she still couldn't get out of her head.. The Reggae
version..

*"It drives me tae Insanity..*
*Cause ah just can't get enough".*

While Madonna ?..Well...She's realised the same as
Rita...And she's thinking......Calvin Harris ??.. Here.!!    .Live
in ma livin' room...??!!   And she was thinking about all the
things her and Calvin were accomplishing in last night's
fantasy.   .Remember I was telling you about that earlier
on?. .And she's wondering if it's too late to Back-Peddle a
good bit?.. Tell B she never meant what she said when she
called her a Hoor..Tell her she really meant she was a

lucky Hoor..That's what she really. Truly meant...
Honestly. ..Hopefully B would understand. .She knows fine
what best pals are like. .They always try and nail each
other to the floor.. Take the utter pish out each other all
the time....Especially pals who were as close as Madge and
Beyoncé were....

But Beyoncé has just new told her wee Braveheart...
.Calvin ..She's fine. But Calvin kens she's no' fine. Because
that's what he asked her..

*"Are ye' share ye'r awright sweetie pie"?*

Beyoncé ..She Sniff.. Sniff.. Sniffs again ..She wipes her
free hand across her eyes .Like she's wiping tears away..

Calvin asks his Sweetie Pie tae tell him what's wrang?

And Rita was wondering if she should maybe go over and
sit down next to her best pal.."B".
Put her arm around her shoulders  ?  ..Just to comfort the
poor Gal..... Or more like just to show Calvin how close B
and her really are....And she's also thinking

*"Ah don't care aboot ma vanity..
Ah love ma love tae kiss ma fluff"..*

.Beyoncé tells Calvin…''*Ah'm jist phonin' tae tell ye'''*. .She says and sniffs another couple of times.. *''There's been a change oh plans. .An' ma.. Ma.. Ma two pals arenae….They're  no' comin' tae Skattland wi' me noo Calvin''*

They hardly heard Calvin ask Sweetie Pie why no?…..Because Madonna jumps out the chair….And she screams..

*''We are sut gawn tae Skatland Calvin''*. She's yelling … .*''We are sut .We've been practicing oor Skattish accent an' awhing… Eh Rita ?''*.

Beyoncé holds the phone nearer her chest.. She knows Madonna would be desperate for Calvin to see her .An' that's jist no' happening.  .No noo anyway. .But then again?. .Then again ?..So she turns her phone round. Look at Madge there. .Just look at her ..She's stopped dead in her tracks. .It's like she's just new walked into a brick wall. .And she's still thinking of everything Calvin and her were getting up to in last night's Fantasy….And she's wishing she wasn't wearing her Joggie bottoms ..Otherwise she would have showed Calvin. .It was her Peach coloured ones she was wearing today…. But she could always lift her top and show Calvin her Tits…Then again. .She couldn't do that. .Could she ?..Naw..Because she'd just new called Beyoncé a Hoor ..Just for doing what Madge wished she had been doing herself.. In the Video...

Rita .She's not wanting Madge to get one over on her. .So she jumps up as well  .. She rushes across the living room . And she's bawling. .*"Aye Calvin.. We are gawn tae Skatland .. We are.. We're gown tae Leslie"*....She's standing right next to Madge now...She was very tempted to shout.. ..*" Ah'll shave ma fanny fir ye' Calvin"*.....She was very temped to burst into the *"Muff Diving Song"*.... .She stops herself though because she wants to hear what Beyoncé's wee Braveheart is saying.

He asks Beyoncé if that's Madge and Rita who are doing all the shouting..?
Beyoncé tells him it is.. Calvin says he can hear them saying they are gawn tae Leslie.....Then Beyoncé.. She sniffs a few more times and tells him that while she was doon at his bit in Noo Yoyk..... The pair had indeed planned to go to Leslie ... But they never even dreamed about inviting her with them..

*"Away tae fuck"* Calvin gasped. .As much in astonishment as amazement.  .*"Ah thought they were ye'r best pals"*?
He asked

219

*"Aye"* Beyoncé sniffed...*"Aye.'"* Then she sniffed again..
*"Ah'm supposed tae be their best pal anyway"*

Before Madge or Rita had the chance to shout it's them
Beyoncé turns to when she's in need....Calvin tells her she
doesn't need pals like that in her life..

Beyoncé. .She sniffs again and sort of half agrees....Then
she tells Calvin that she feels such a stupid fool for even
considering these pair in her own plans....

This was true...Oh yeah...When Calvin had first suggested
she should come and live in Paradise Park......She'd agreed
gladly.....The idea had seemed great at first...Then after a
few days , when she'd had a wee bit of time to think
about things seriously... .She thought there was only so
much time you could spend in Calvin's Gym or indoor
swimming pool .  She'd told Calvin that she'd maybe get
fed up padding about his Mansion on her own when he
was away on tour.....
Calvin had promised her Dougray..Gerard an' that wid nip
round noo and again.. And that wiz aw fine ..Oh Gawd
yeah...Fine and Dandy.....But still....It's no' the same as
havin' ye'r auld pals aroond aboot ye'....She really wanted
her  best pals to have a taste of the action.......And as I've
not long told you...Beyoncé had mentioned this to
Calvin......He gladly proposed bringing her auld pals ower

tae Scotland..... And you already know what two pals Beyoncé had chosen.. Don't you ??.....

Calvin tells her not to worry ..He tells her not to put herself down. ..She'd done the right thing by her pals....Absolutely the right thing...That's the kind of things best pals do for each other he tells her........He assures her It wasn't her fault they weren't as kind hearted as her and hadn't considered asking her to go with them ........

He asks her to cheer up and says she'll make plenty pals when she gets tae Leslie...*"Real pals"* He says... .He then asks her to think about all the Scottish friends she's made already. .And she's not even stepped foot in the country yet...Beyoncé feels a wee bit better hearing Calvin say this ..Ever since they first met.. He'd had that uplifting effect on her. .Even when she'd divulged to him about how traumatised she'd been about the death of *"Goldielocks"*.......Calvin had not only sympathised with her. He'd empathised with her as well...Because. .Just the other year.. He'd been in the same boat after he'd lost his pet Hamster ..*"Hammy"*.. He'd been in an awfy state about that....Been on the phone tae The Samaritans and awhing... .He confided in Beyoncé that *"Hammy"* and him had what could only be described as a spiritual connection.... *Just the very same as Beyoncé and*

"*Goldielocks*"..Then .One sunny evening...After making Luv  beneath the palm trees in the
garden of Calvin's Noo Yoyk Mansion...They had wrote the first verse of a song dedicated to both Hammy and Goldielocks. .She couldn't remember the tune Calvin had made up...But thought she could mind the words....If she remembers rightly ..It went..

*"Goldielocks and Hammy.. We wish you didn't have to die.*
*But Goldielocks and Hammy ..Now live up in the sky*
*And Goldielocks and Hammy wouldn't want us both to cry...                                   But Goldielocks*
*and Hammy.. We miss you more than words can say..*

Then she remembered a wee bit of the chorus..

*But to try an' tell yooz how we feel....*
*We miss Hammy birlin' on her wheel. .*
*We miss Goldie swmmin' in her bowl..*
*May God bless and keep your soul..*

Calvin had said that if they get another verse or two?.. Then he would ask one of his other Skattish pals ..Nicola Benedetti.. To play the violin on the song.. He promised it would be a bigger hit than Elvis Presley's *"Old Shep"*..About the death of his trusty dog....

Madge shouts to Calvin they had planned their big trip tae Skatland while Beyoncé was away doon in Noo Yoyk..

' "Oh ! 'Is that right ?' Calvin asks....And Beyoncé was just on the verge of telling him they never included her in their plans to go to Australia either. .But Rita yells..

She yells to Calvin that Beyoncé was away for a whole fortnight and they thought she'd found Tru-Luv with the Artist.. She also shouts that they were worried seek about her..

"Is *that right*" ? Asks Calvin again.....

"*Aye*...It is right...Madge agrees.. .*Worried seek'*... *We were goin' tae phone the Polis an' awhing*"

And Calvin?...Once more he asks if that's right..?...

"*Aye it's right*". Rita shouts " *Gawn tae report her missin' an' awhing*" '*An' that's jist cause Beyoncé's  oor best pal* ?..

And Calvin?.. He hesitates a second before replying...But when he does. .He says. .'
'*Well. .If Beyoncé's that close a pal?* He tells them.'*Yooz could have phoned her couldn't ye*"?

Sha Hoor Sir.. That fairly put Madge and Rita's Gas at a peep…..What could they say in reply to Calvin's statement eh ?   Nothing. !!   .Because he was right…Aye he was right. .They could have phoned her…..But look at them…...The wind has been taken out of their sails..... And the big thing is.. They had no intention of reporting Beyoncé missing. .None at all. ..As you already know.. They had been wondering what she was up to?   Oh aye….But as for reporting her missing ?..They both turn round..

Beyoncé turns her phone round…

Calvin winks..
She winks back…

Calvin licks his forefinger and makes an invisible mark in thin air…''One up'', he's saying silently.. …Beyoncé winks again….Aye… One up……

On Beyoncé hearing Calvin say about them not phoning her………She felt that big guilty weight lift right off her shoulders.. He was right. .Oh aye…She felt like she was enjoying herself again. .Enjoying seeing the nails being driven in …  And it wasn't even her who was yielding the hammer.

*Maybe it was Beyoncé's Manic-Ness I was telling you about earlier at work?. Up and down like a Yo-Yo.. .Who knows ? Although she'd been crying just a minute ago...The tears had stopped.. This Gal was on her way up again.....*

The other pair have flop themselves back down on their chairs ..Like puppets who have had their strings cut...Then Beyoncé tells Calvin she'd ripped up all the tickets for the flight tae Skatland....Aye Calvin had paid for Beyoncé and her two best pals flights ....British Airways...First class. .Flying Non-Stop... Straight into the Arlene Duffy International Airport......Everything the other pair had been dreaming about..

She thought Calvin would be angry, but he tells her she's quite right and he's glad she's ripped them up..... He says these pair of selfish so and so's don't deserve to have pal like her...Once again. .Calvin was right...She had no need to put herself on a guilt trip because of these two. .No need whatsoever.......Because. .Well. .How many times had she asked if they were taking her to Skatland with them ? ...Five. .Six maybe?...And what had been their answer every single time she'd asked?.. Fuck off.. .And just to think. .All the pleading she'd done with Calvin. .Just to get her best pals over to Skatland with her..

Then Calvin asks about the tickets for the Lad-Zone concert?
She tells him she's ripped all them up anaw…..And the ones for the Leslie Hearts.. Barcelona game..
She thought he really would be angry on hearing this. .Because it had been some task to get these tickets…..But Calvin had managed…He'd got Beyoncé and her two best pals tickets for the bands comeback concert as well as tickets for the big game…….. .
Their seats were the best seats in the Belladrome as well… In the John Forrest Memorial stand….
As you already know.. Madge and Rita had been dreaming about exactly the same thing….Hadn't they ?

Calvin. .Once more tells Beyoncé she's quite right… He's going on about how thousands of Gals would love to have a pal who's as considerate as Beyoncé was. .While he's talking. Beyoncé swipes all the ripped up pieces of the envelopes into the copper waste paper basket.. That'll be the tickets then eh ?..

And I'm sure I don't need to explain what Madge and Rita are thinking eh no'?.. You can see the look on their faces for yourself…And that says it all…The tickets

ripped up an' awhing....In the fuckin' bucket.......No
wonder they're looking sick eh ?......No wonder they're
sitting there not saying a word. The wind has been
taken right out their sails.......But Beyoncé's
thinking..Aye..Yooz pair are seek noo eh ?. Well fuck
ye'z ..She thought...No more Mrs nice Gal....
They didn't feel the least bit guilty about not inviting her
tae Skatland.. Did they?.. .

Rita's hoping Calvin will ask about  the Muff Diving song.
.She is. .She's hoping Beyoncé will tell him that Madge
says it was shite.. Utter shite.. Rita's hoping for all this
because she might have a wee chance to redeem
herself. .Tell Calvin it was only Madge who said
that…...But she thought the song was brilliant. .Beyoncé
doesn't mention the song though ..But she does
mention the Video.....
You'll have noticed Beyoncé wiping away another tear
there... She's away again…...Greetin'....And she's tellin'
Calvin that Madonna says she was nothin' but a Hoor
for videoing her shagging Dougray and his pals.....She
sniffs another two or three times and wipes another
tear away..

Calvin couldn't believe what she was saying... .He tells
Beyoncé that she only got it videoed tae show her pals
what wiz in store when they came ower tae Scotland..

'Ah ken'' Beyoncé sniffs .''Ah ken Calvin.. Ma wee
BraveHeart.....But. .But ..But she still says ah'm a Hoor''

Calvin never got the opportunity to reply....... .Because
Rita saw her chance and took it.....She jumps up...''Ah
never says she wiz a Hoor Calvin'' She bawls and rushes
over to where Beyoncé's sitting...''Ah never says she wiz
a Hoor Calvin.'' ..She repeats...And she's trying to get
Calvin to see her... But Beyoncé keeps turning her
phone away.....''It wiz Madge that says she wiz a Hoor ''
She shouts...'''No me''....She was just about to
shout..''Ah'll shave ma Fanny fir ye'Calvin'' She was.
.Then after that she planned to... burst into the Muff
diving song in the hope that Calvin would adore her
singing skills.... She was...It was just on the tip of her
tongue...But Madge jumps up as well....The anger's
pouring out her..

''Ah thought You're supposed tae be ma fuckin best' pal ?''
She roars at Rita..'

It's like we're going to get a fight after all. .Because in four
big mad steps Madge is over.. She pushes Rita and asks
her the question again.
Rita pushes her back ..''Don't you push me aboot '' She
shouts...She was just about to swear. .But

dizznae...Instead she shouts......"*Ah'm both your pals*"...
.Well... She is wanting Calvin to hear her isn't she ?.So
she shouts even louder still... "*Ah'm both you'r pals.. Eh
Beyonce*"?  She asks..."*An' we shouldnae be arguing
like this*"..

And Beyoncé. .She's still greetin' intae her phone...Calvin's
tellin' Beyoncé no' tae greet......

'*Aw come on ma wee Honey* Suckle" He's saying
soothingly..."*Dinnae Greet ower the Heed oh yon pair*" .

Madonna.. She pushes Rita again. .'*Aye*" She says and
goes to grab Rita's hair. .But Rita leans back out the
road…. ."*Aye*" .Madge repeats..". *Ye' must think ah'm
fuckin' daft eh ?*  She points at Beyoncé and
shouts..."*You're kissin' up that Cannts  erse aren't ye?
*"...

Madge is staring straight at Beyoncé now and if Rita just
lifts her foot quickly. .She could kick Madge right in the
Fanny. .She doesn't do it though. .For one reason.. And
one reason only???....

Calvin asks who's doing all the swearing ?  Beyoncé sniffs
a couple of times and tells him... It's Madge...

*''Sha Hoor Sir''* Calvin replies..*''Sha Hoor sir.. She's got a mooth on her that wan.eh''* ?

Beyoncé doesn't get a chance to say a word…Because Madge gets in their first….
*''Aye.''* .She shouts in fury ….*'' Aye.. Ah have got a fuckin' Mooth on me''* She shouts. .*''That's why the Guys aw cry me…Dyson''*..

*''Dyson''* Calvin laughs *''Dyson ?.*

*''Aye Dyson''* Madge snaps…

Then…Just like he had all his answer made up…Calvin replies…*''Is that cause ye sook crumbs up aff the flair''*?

Beyoncé laughs as well. .Like I was saying. .Up and down like a Yo_Yo.

While Rita. .She has to laugh doesn't she ?..Because she's more of a  close pal to Beyoncé isn't she ?. Oh she's wanting to keep in with Beyoncé alright..
Madge isn't laughing though. .Oh no…Once more she asks Rita just who's fuckin' pal she is?...Then without waiting on an answer, she shouts at Calvin….*''No it's no' cause ah sook crumbs aff the flair''* She roars. .*''It's cause ah*

*give a better B.J. than any other Gal roond aboot here''..*

Rita was going to shout something in disagreement. .But? … Wasn't she acting as the peacemaker..?.. She didn't want Calvin to hear her arguing did she? …That's why she didn't kick Madge in the Fanny when she'd tried to grab her hair…….She's thinking if things work out as planned ?..Then she'll maybe get the chance to show Calvin and aw his pals just how good at giving a B.J. she is.. Much better than that Madonna Hoor anyway..

The Calvin one's on the ball though…Oh aye.. Well ..These two needn't bother thinking they're making a fool of his new Gal……He tells Madge she couldn't give a better B.J. than his wee Honey Bun… Beyoncé. .He says aw his pals will back him up on that one..

Beyoncé's spirits were sky high now…Sky high…. Her wee Braveheart eh ?.Just listen to him there…What a romantic thing to say about somebody…
When she'd told Calvin he was the Ying to her Yang.. She was right..

But Madge wasn't taking that kind of talk from anybody…Calvin Harris or no' Calvin Harris…*''Away an' shut ye'r puss''* She yells. .

*''Away an 'shut ye'r ain puss''* .Calvin replies and laughs…. Madge tells him she's no' shuttin' her puss for the likes of him…Then she tells him that aw his Movie star pals will soon change their minds when her and Rita get their gums around their plums..

*''Oh dae ye' hink you'll be meetin' aw ma pals''* ? Calvin laughed even louder.. …

Madge assured him they most definitely would.. *''We're gawn tae cowp them aw''*.. She tells him and asks Rita to back her up, but Rita doesn't get the chance to reply.. Because Calvin tells her that she's got a hard neck calling Beyoncé a Hoor… Then he laughs louder still.….This. .Too Madge.. Was like a red rag to a Bull…*''An' we're getting' oor ain tickets tae the Lad-Zone concert ''*..She roars…*''And tae the Barcelona game anaw''*

*''Oh are ye'' ?* Calvin laughed.*.'' Imagine that ?''*

*''We're no' imaginin' fuck all''* .Madge tells him.. *''Me an' Rita' be there awright''*

*''Oh will ye noo ? ''* Calvin asked through his laughter….

*''Aye will we noo''* Madge told him…*''So we dinnae need you ya' Skattish Caannt''*. .Once again she asks Rita to

back her up.. And once again. .Rita doesn't get the chance. Because Calvin changes tact...He tells Beyoncé he doesn't know why she's hanging about with such a pair of self- cantered Hoors.....He says he could tell they were only interested in themselves...It sticks oot a mile he tells her......He says she's far too kind a person for false pals like them....He tells her folk like them will just drag her down......They're a bad influence he tells her...*And he didn't even know about them scamming the catalogues. .Neither did he know they were both growing weed for Barry Bang..Bang.*...But Beyoncé.... She just starts greetin' again.. She does.. Although she knew fine Calvin was talking the truth... She couldn't help herself becoming emotional.....

Calvin's tellin' his wee Sugar pumpkin no' tae greet.....He's sayin' that he's jist tellin' her the truth.. She's needin' tae leave folk like them behind her...Forget aw aboot them. .Beyoncé's still sniff..Sniff..Sniffin'...She's sayin' she kens fine he's talkin' perfect sense.....
Calvin tells her she's got a great future ahead of her in the music industry.. Just wait till she gets tae Leslie he says...

*''Aye Calvin''* Was all Beyoncé said In reply...She sniffs another few times. .Then tells him she'll get awfy fed up paddin' aboot his Mansion for 3 weeks until he comes back from his tour..

Calvin tells her he's been thinking about that.. He tells her he's missin' her awfy…..Beyoncé.. She sniffs and tells Calvin she's missin' him awfy anaw…Calvin hesitates a few seconds then he asks if Beyoncé would fancy coming on tour with him ?..Then Beyoncé really did burst out greetin'..

*"Oh aye… That wid be great Calvin"* She greets .*"Fantastic"* She sniffs another couple of times. .*".Great"*


As you know.. Madge and Rita were standing listening to all this. .They didn't stand long though..
Madge stares at Rita…
Rita stares right back..
Madge nods her head in Beyoncé's direction. .Remember she's sitting with the tears blinding her. Tears of happiness this time though..
Both the other pair turn on their heels. .They flop themselves back down on their chairs..
And they're listening to Beyoncé telling Calvin that would be great..
Although Madge and Rita are sitting listening ..The Telepathy was at work again..
Madge is thinking..*"Dinnae worry Ree..That Hoor thinks we're jealous"*…

And Ree is thinking in reply.''.*Fuckin' right Madge. .We'll show them what B.J.s an' shaggin's aw aboot when we get tae Leslie eh "*?

Meanwhile.. Calvin's telling Beyoncé he cannae wait tae see her again.. Cannae wait... .And Beyoncé?  ...She's wiped aw the tears away now...The Gals don't know she's just remembered that she's supposed to be enjoying herself. ...Watching the nails being hammered in.. She tells Calvin she cannae wait tae see him either...

And I don't have to explain what was going on over the Telepathic airwaves eh no'? ..Imagine thinking thoughts like that.... And Beyoncé is supposed to be there best pal..??

But Calvin's just new told Beyoncé he'll phone Floyd right away and just get him to turn back and pick her up again.... ..
Beyoncé says he can land the Helicopter on the school playing field across the road from her house...Aye ..She's going back to her own place to pick some things up she explains.. She'll get a Cab over. .Even though she lived only a ten minute walk away. .She didn't fancy carrying all those bags full of new claes shoes etc...

And the Telepathic airwaves are on fire. .These pair shouldn't be hoping the Helicopter would crash. .Gee. .Beyoncé and them were the closest of friends weren't they?   .Aye. .But Calvin wasn't easy kidded on was he..??..He'd twigged on.. So Naw..They couldn't really claim to be her closest friend after all….

So after a good minute and a half of Calvin and Beyoncé debating about who was going to put the phone down first. .And after all the Koochie---Koos..And the I Love Yooz..And the kisses blown…The call eventually ends….Like love-struck teenagers…And even though the other pair wanted to say anything…They never had a chance, Because Beyoncé phones a Cab right away…...Soon as possible please she asks…Two or three minutes would be just great…... Yes indeed.. She gave Madge's address..   Going to  her own address…Thank you…That phone call ends and Beyoncé starts gathering up her stuff.. She puts her phone.. Her weed Etc back in her M.K. Handbag…She slips her shades back on… Then stands up….She lifts all the bags of clothes..

''*Is that you away then B*''? Rita asks feeling a tear swell up…. She felt like the very least she could do is give B a Goodbye cuddle.. And maybe ask if it would be O.K. if they could visit Calvin when they were in Leslie?

*''Aye that's her away''* Madge answered.. *''The Hoor's too good fir the likes oh us Noo Ree....*

Beyoncé knew Madge's game though.. Of course she did. .But she wasn't biting.. No way.

*''Her auld pals'll jist drag her doon..''* .Madge continued.'' *She'd prefer swannin' aboot wi' aw they Famous folk noo''*

But Beyoncé was high again. .Madge could use words as bullets all she liked... Beyoncé felt bulletproof...Arguing with Madge might put her back on a downer....
Oh.. She could shout that Jealousy will get Madge nowhere and you've got to admit.. The jealousy is pouring out of her eh ?  . ..
Beyoncé could shout  that she'll be swanin' aboot wi' even more famous folk when Calvin and her are away on tour...But Na .Although she had a few choice words to say to these pair. .She'd wait a minute or two before telling them.....At the moment, she wasn't giving Madge the pleasure of reacting to her poison...And Madge doesn't like this. Does she ?

*''Ye'd better get gawn then ''* Madge growled with even more venom....*''Floyd'll be here in the Helicopter shortly'''*
..

*"Oh ! Right enough. "* Beyoncé replied .Trying to sound surprised...*"Right enough ..Ah nearly forgot aboot that"* She drops the bags of clothes.. She slips her red frilly knickers off again. .She winks and drops her knickers into her M.K. Handbag.. .

Sha Hoor Sir. . That's truly has sickened Rita and Madge eh?. .Just look at the pair of them there.....What words would you use to describe the look on their
 faces ??  .And by this time...You know fine what they'll be thinking as well eh?..Aye..Ah'll bet you do...

*"Away an' raffle"* Madge roared at Beyoncé. .*"Away an' raffle"*......Then she told Rita not to worry and they'll meet much better folk than Calvin Harris when they get tae Skatland....But Rita already knew this didn't she ?  ......Oh Gawd yeah...

*"Ach. .Away an' Byle ye'r Heeds"* Beyoncé told them.. *"Away an' Byle ye'r Heeds"*..

*"What dae ye' mean?...Byle oor Heeds"* Madge questioned..

*"Jist what ah'm sayin"* Beyoncé answered..*"Byle ye'r Heeds"*

Then Beyoncé really does get all starry eyed and dreamlike……..''*It's a Skattish sayin'*''..She explains and flickers her eyelids….. .''*Ah must have picked it up spendin' too much time around aw they sexy Skattish Actors an' that ..An it means…Fuck off. !!!   The baith oh ye'z*''.

''*Us*''? Madge responded  ''*We're no' fuckin' off anywhere*''

''*Exactly*''  Beyoncé snapped back..''*Eck..Fuckin' Zaktly…Nae where.*''…

''*Except Skatland like*'' Rita added..

Beyoncé turns and points at Rita. .'…*Yooz two caannts'll never go near Skatland or anywhere else*'' .She says…..*Ah'll tell ye' what's gawn tae happen…See If ah come back next year.? .Yooz two will still be cuttin' aboot the hoose in ye'r Baffies an' Joggie bottoms….Yez'll still be rubbin' the Fanny's aff yersels…..Fantasisin' aboot ridin' aw they Movie stars…Yez'll hiv ye'r Fanny's rubbed red raw..*

''*Will we fuck*'' Rita replied.. ''*We'll be ridin' plenty Movie stars ..Eh Madge ?*'' ..But Madge never had the chance to answer cause Beyoncé's on a roll… ''*You two'll Sit aw day.*

*.An' aw night''*...She tells them..."*Smokin' weed...Yez'll Travel the world''* She says..."'*The hale wide fuckin' world. .An' never leave ye'r living room''*.... She's got her hands on her hips now. .And she's giving her two Ex best pals it good style.... *''Livin' ye'r life in ye'r ain Heed...That's you two''* She tells them*. ....*

Madge was just about to deny this.. But Beyoncé rants on. .She asks if Barry Bang Bang would ever let them out of his clutches? ..The other pair never got the chance to reply to this question either, because Beyoncé bursts out into a loud ..Mad Manic laugh.. But the other two never knew the reason for her laughing was to stop her bursting out greeting again...And just to think. .A second or two ago.. Her heart felt lighter than a Hobo's holdall....But through the laughter that's hiding her tears.. She's shouting..."*And you've the hard neck tae say it's me that's livin' in Alice in Wonderland??.....Ah'm livin' in Fantasy land ???.....*Then she stops laughing and starts singing .."*Travel The Wo-orld an' never leave ye'r livin' room...... Barry Bang Bangs slaves .Barry Bang Bangs slaves .Rub the Fanny's aff yersels..Rub the fanny's aff yersels....''*

Madge jumps up..."*Ach away you an'shut ye'r puss''* She yells over the top of Beyoncé's own wee tune.

Beyoncé stops her reverie and tells Madge to shut her ain puss..

*"Ach away you an' byle ye're Heed"* Madge shouts in reply.." *"Fuck off"'.!!!*

Beyoncé. .She gets right in Madge's face…. Sha Hoor sir.. They've been talkin' like real Skatswoman..And Noo..They're arguing like real Skatswoman anaw..Right in each others pusses…Nose to nose they are…I'm expecting a kiss. .Glasgow style…What aboot you ?......
*"That's jist what ah'm dane Madge doll"* Beyoncé smiles…" *Ah'm Fuckin' off. !! Right off !!   .Oot the road oh you two selfish Caannts…Skatland..Here we come"*

Maybe there would have been a Glasgow kiss coming. ? .But the Taxi has just peeped it's horn three times…*"Todd's Taxi"*. As reliable as ever......Beyoncé turns around…She  lifts her bags of clothes and without another word being said. .Without a Goodbye cuddle or nothing for her Ex best pals.. She brushes past Madge and marches straight out the living room. And still…. Madge never had the chance to have a good squint to see what was in the bags…

*''Aye.. Fuck off then''* Madge shouts at Beyoncé's retreating figure. *.''Leave ye'r best pals..Ya Trollop that ye' are''*

As it was obvious there was no chance of Rita becoming Beyoncé's best pal now. ..And just to forget about never getting away from the clutches of Barry Bang..Bang….She jumps up and starts shouting as well..

*''Aye''* She shouts…*''Too good fir the likes oh us noo eh ?...Well ah hope ye' get a dose ya Hoory Caannt that ye' are. ''*

Beyoncé doesn't even close Madge's front door.. And you can hear her high heels click. .Click. .Clicking on the landing. ( *Sounding very much like The Lord Mayor of Leslie when he's walking across the laminate flooring in his own high heels.*)….And the other two are now at Madge's living room door.. Shouting all those horrible things along the lobby…But this doesn't bother the Beyoncé one.. No chance…She's leaving them behind…She's off to start a new life altogether….A new life with Calvin in Bonnie Skatland..And it wouldn't just be anywhere in Skatland….It would be in Leslie…Paterson Park.. Just imagine. .Paterson Park ??  …So.. Just to get it right up these pair of selfish. .Jealous dreamers for one final time… She just starts singing again.. But it's not her own wee tune she's singing as she walks down the stairs...It's not *''The Muff Diving Song''* either..... No. She bursts into that song ...That beautiful Skattish song she'd heard all those men singing when she'd been sitting all the long lonely hours by the waterside in Noo Yoyk..When she'd been thinking about jumping in and drooning herself to death....

*''I Don't know if you can see.. The changes that have come over me''* She sang proudly......Just listen to her there.. Does that not sound just truly beautiful ?..Goodness me. ..That sounds as beautiful as the Angels themselves singing....And that song fairly sets your heart alight eh ?...Oh aye....It fair the hairs on ye'r neck stand tae attention eh ?..But ah'd better shut ma ain puss a wee while because ye'll be wantin' tae hear Beyoncé singing one of your favourite songs... Eh ?..You can even join in if you fancy?.. Nobody will phone the polis on you for singing this song. .Because no matter where about in this world you're listening to this story...It'll likely be these officer favourite song anaw... They'll maybe ask you to sing it again so as they can sing along...So sing it louder and sing it prouder than when you were singing the Muff Diving Song.. Are you ready?.. Here we go then..

*"These last few days. .I've been afraid that I might drift away..*

*So I've been telling stories .Singing songs ..*
*That make me think about where I came from...*
*That's the reason why I seem so far away today..*

*Oh won't you let me tell you that I love you ..*
*And I think about you all the time...Caledonia you're*
*calling me...*

## CHAPTER 4

## THE STORIES END

Then they hear the close door slamming shut. .And they
never heard Beyoncé sing any more. .Madge nips quickly
along the lobby.. She shuts and locks the front door. .By
the time she's back in the living room. .Rita is standing at
the window .Madge joins her.. To watch *"Todd"* The taxi
driver, loading Beyoncé's bags into the boot of his
cab...Beyoncé didn't even look up to wave goodbye to her
old pals as she opened the passenger side door ..She
stepped in and closed the door...They would maybe never
see Beyoncé in their lives again.. And she couldn't even be
bothered to wave goodbye.. Aye. .Well..

*''Well no' miss that moochin' faced Hoor anyway .Eh no'*
*Ree ''*? Madge asked and started flicking the Veez down at
Beyoncé.. With both hands..

244

*"Na. .Will we hell"* Ree answered..*" We'll no miss the likes oh her"..* She copies Madge ..Flicking the Veez..With both hands..

But they both knew they would miss her. .Not as much as they would miss each other. But aye. They would miss Beyoncé.. Because. .In the few years they had known her, and despite her Manic-Ness and her O.C.D behaviour, they really did have some rare old laughs together.. Taking the utter piss out each other aw the time.. The pelters flying back and forward faster than swallows on a summers evening.. .But that's what you do with your pals eh?..

Oh but here. .She's out.. She's out again.. The Roving Reporter's running down her path at top fluffy pink Baffie speed. ..Can you see her there ?....Her Binoculars are still hanging round her neck.. She's too late to spear the arse out Beyoncé though because the Taxi has just drawn away....And putting her binoculars up to her eyes won't bring Beyoncé back either...She's so disgusted by her lateness. .Oh she's mad alright. .What a juicy story she could have got.. Ach.. Still. .She could always add arms and legs to what she already knew..... She turns on her heels and heads back into her house.. Never once even looking up at Madge and Rita. She slams her front door shut in anger and frustration..

*"At least we're still best pals though Ree"*? Madge stated ..Feeling glad that Rita's attempts to kiss up Beyoncé's arse had been futile. .But she'd talk to her about that later on..

*"Aye"* Was all Rita said in reply. .But she's thinking. Well. .She's thinking a lot of things.. One of them is.. How the hell do I get out the clutches of Barry Bang. .Bang?

*'An' 'Imagine that Calvin Caannt sayin' we'd drag Beyoncé doon "* Madge continues

*"Ah ken"* Rita answers*.."Soonds like a right cheeky Caannt eh?.. "*?..Although she's saying this. .She still couldn't help herself imagining Calvin and her. .Naked in his swimming pool..

*"Ayr ,,But..Dinnae you worry".* .Madge assures her and stops flicking the Veez.......*"The first time that mad Hoor takes wan oh her Skitzo turns.. Her arse'll be oot the winndae"*

*"Right oot"*..Rita agrees and stops flicking the Veez as well.... *"Calvin'll no' put up wi' that Pshyco cows shite fir long wance she starts smashin' his Mansion up'"*...

But Rita's also wondering if Beyoncé's arse will be out the winndae by the time her and Madge reach Leslie?....If so ?..Calvin will be looking for a new Burd won't he ? ..Maybe a new singer for The Muff Diving Song?. .The song that's still going round in her head.

*"Oh let your tongue explore ma pussy*
*Make ma piss flaps braw an' juicy."*

And as you know already. .If Rita is thinking all this? Then so is Madge.. Not a word about it spoken between them though...

To take her mind off smiling at the image of Beyoncé sitting selling *"The Big Issue"* in Leslie.. Madge asks if Rita was still hungry?

*" Hank Marvin"* Rita answers. .*"Ah could eat a scabby Horse sandwiched between two pishy mattresses.*

*"Me tae'* 'Madge laughed. *"But only if it had salad cream on it"* .

*"It's an Italian dish ye'r makin' eh ?* Rita asks as Madge heads for the kitchen..

Madge tells her it is indeed an Italian delicacy......And Rita asks what exactly the Italian delicacy was.?. Madge answers it's Ravioli on toast..

*''Ravioli on toast''* Rita gasps. *.''Ah thought it wiz a delicacy ye' were makin'?..*

*"It is a fuckin' delicacy ya cheeky Caannt.."* Madge stops in her tracks and turns to face Rita*...; ''There's folk in Biafra wid cut ye'r throat fir some Ravioli''* She says. *.''Especially if it's Heinz''....*

*"Aye. .Right enough''* Rita agrees. Because she knew fine if she refused Madge's Italian delicacy?.... Then they would have to go through to Rita's place.. And Rita would have to do the cooking. .She's a fly wan the Madge eh *?....* *''Aye ..Right enough''. .*Rita repeats... Then asks if Madge has ever been to Italy..?

The answer was that although her granny and grand-Pappy were both Italian. Madge had never been near the place.... She asks what Rita's probing for?

Rita answers it's just because Italian Dudes are Randy as fuck.. She smiles at the Memories of all the Italian Stallions she'd met in her time...

*''Sha Hoor aye ..They are that..''* Madge agrees ..She also smiles as her mind drifts back to the very same memories. *''.No' half ''* .

*'Well Imagine''* Rita says... *''Imagine ..You an' me in Italy. Eh? ....Oui..Oui Môn sour,,.. You take us up zee Eiffel tower anytime''..*

*''The Eiffel tower?''* Madge asks. *''.The Eiffel tower's in France ya daft Hoor''..*

*''Is it'* Rita asks in all seriousness.. *''France''?. .*

*''Aye''* Madge replies.. *''It's in Paris.. An' Paris is in France''..*

*''Ah'll Google it ''*Rita says.. She takes a few steps towards where her tablet lay.. The screen will have went to sleep by this time.. But if she taps it awake. You'll find out who that Hunk who's near naked torso had been staring out at them. .Remember at the very start of the story?.. .She stops in her tracks when Madge tells her..

*"There's nae need tae Google anything. ."Cause ah'm tellin' ye'.. The Eiffel tower's in Paris...An' Paris is in France"..*

*"Well"* ..Says Rita then asks *."How far is France fae Skatland?*

*"Fuck knows"* Madonna answers. *".What are ye' askin' that fir like?*

*"Naw "*Says Rita. .*"It's jist that wance we've been tae Skatland...We could maybe could go tae Fra"* ..Then all of a sudden. Just like she'd had an Electric shock or something.. She stops talking ...She stares at Madge.. And she bursts out laughing..

Madge bursts out laughing as well

They both open their arms wide and take a step forward to cuddle each other...

And they're laughing so much.. The tears are in their eyes. .Listen to the pair of them laughing. .It's like they've just heard the best joke ever.. And in a funny way. .I suppose they have......Because.... In their Heart of Hearts. .They both knew...They knew fine.. Beyoncé was right....Every

word. .They were living in Fantasy land. .But who cares?  .
They were having a great time..

# THE END.

So that's it Ladies and Gentlemen. Another story told and
thank-you very much for taking the time to sit and
listen…Above it all, I hope you've had a right good
laugh.. If you would like your friends and loved ones
either at home or abroad to enjoy it as well.. Then
please tell them, this book is also available on Kindle
and a paperback copy can be ordered from the Amazon
bookstore. .Thanks once again.. Michael Kelly..

23224278R00149

Printed in Great Britain
by Amazon